Taran Wanderer

YEARLING BOOKS BY LLOYD ALEXANDER YOU WILL ENJOY:

THE PRYDAIN CHRONICLES:
THE BOOK OF THREE
THE BLACK CAULDRON
THE CASTLE OF LLYR
TARAN WANDERER
THE HIGH KING

YEARLING BOOKS are designed especially to entertain and enlighten young people. Patricia Reilly Giff, consultant to this series, received her bachelor's degree from Marymount College and a master's degree in history from St. John's University. She holds a Professional Diploma in Reading and a Doctorate of Humane Letters from Hofstra University. She was a teacher and reading consultant for many years, and is the author of numerous books for young readers.

TARAN WANDERER

by Lloyd Alexander

A YEARLING BOOK

For Wayfarers still journeying,
for Wanderers at rest.

Published by
Bantam Doubleday Dell Books for Young Readers
a division of
Bantam Doubleday Dell Publishing Group, Inc.
1540 Broadway
New York, New York 10036

ISBN: 0-440-48483-9

Reprinted by arrangement with Holt, Rinehart and Winston, Inc.

Printed in the United States of America

One Previous Edition

April 1990

30   29   28   27

OPM

Contents

Author's Note

This fourth chronicle of Prydain begins as a gallant, high-hearted quest, which soon becomes more intense and perhaps more essentially heroic than the preceding adventures. For here, Taran comes to grips with a merciless opponent: the truth about himself. No longer as Taran Assistant Pig-Keeper but as Taran Wanderer, he learns to reshape his life out of his own inner resources; for there must not only be an end to childhood but also a beginning of manhood. This is meant to be a serious tale—in the way that all humor is serious and all fantasy true—and if there is no conventionally happy ending in fairy-tale terms, there is still a most hopeful ending in human terms.

This does not imply any less humor or variety in the story. There is possibly more, as Taran's journey takes him from one end of Prydain to the other, from the Marshes of Morva to the Free Commots. However, instead of a clash of battle hosts, the underlying conflict between good and evil is stated in individual encounters: King Smoit, boisterous with being alive; Morda, deathlike, scornful of all humanity; Dorath the amoral; Annlaw Clay-Shaper the creator; Craddoc, in whose desolate valley Taran suffers the anguish of shame. The Princess Eilonwy, alas, is present only in memory, though it is hoped readers will miss her as much as Taran does—and the author himself, for that matter.

While certain inhabitants of Prydain were born of Welsh legend, in *Taran Wanderer* they have acquired characteristics more universal than specific. Morda's life secret, for example, is familiar in many mythologies. Orddu, Orwen, and Orgoch have appeared in other guises (as might well be expected of them): the Three Norns, the Moirae, the Triple Goddess, and very likely some other transformations they decline to admit. Prydain, of course, is part-memory and part-dream, the balance favoring the latter.

The Companions have gained many more friends than I had ever hoped, who are willing to follow these tales both as self-contained chronicles and as part of a larger pattern; and to them I promise in time all questions will be answered and all secrets revealed. To some friends of the Companions (especially Gypsy Reeves) I address a plea for clemency; to others, my sincere thanks for their hard but invaluable labor, insight, and encouragement when the straits seemed even more dire to an author than to an Assistant Pig-Keeper; and to all, my warmest affection.

—L.A.

CHAPTER I

Who am I?

t was full springtime, with promise of the richest summer the farm had ever seen. The orchard was white with fragrant blossoms; the newly planted fields lay light as green mist. Yet the sights and scents gave Taran little joy. To him, Caer Dallben was empty. Though he helped Coll with the weeding and cultivating, and tended the white pig, Hen Wen, with as much care as ever, he went about his tasks distractedly. One thought alone was in his mind.

"Now, my boy," Coll said good-naturedly, as they finished the morning's milking, "I've seen you restless as a wolf on a tether ever since you came back from the Isle of Mona. Pine for the Princess Eilonwy if you must, but don't upset the milk pail." The stout old warrior clapped Taran on the shoulder. "Come, cheer up. I'll teach you the high secrets of planting turnips. Or raising cabbages. Or whatever you might want to know."

Taran shook his head. "What I would know only Dallben can tell me."

"Take my counsel, then," said Coll. "Trouble 9

Dallben with none of your questions. His thoughts are on deeper matters. Have patience and bide your time."

Taran rose to his feet. "I can bide my time no longer. It is in my heart to speak with him now."

"Have a care," warned Coll as Taran strode to the door of the shed. "His disposition rubs a little thin!"

Taran made his way through the cluster of low-roofed farm buildings. In the cottage, at the hearth-side, a black-robed woman crouched and tended the cooking fire. She did not raise her head or speak. It was Achren. Thwarted in her scheme to regain her ancient power, from the ruined Castle of Llyr the once-haughty Queen had accepted the refuge Dall-ben offered; though, by her own choice, she who had long ago ruled Prydain toiled now at the tasks Eilonwy had done before departing for Mona, and at day's end silently vanished to her pallet of straw in the granary.

Before Dallben's chamber Taran paused un-easily, then rapped quickly on the door. Entering at the enchanter's command, he found Dallben bent over *The Book of Three*, which lay open on the cluttered table. Much as he longed for a glimpse at even one page of this secret volume, Taran kept his distance from it. Once, in boyhood, he had dared touch the ancient, leather-bound tome, and his fingers smarted again at the memory.

"I never cease to wonder," Dallben testily remarked, closing *The Book of Three* and glancing at Taran, "that the young, with all their pride of strength, should find their own concerns such a weighty burden they must be shared with the old. Whereas, the old"—he waved a frail, bony hand. "But no matter, no matter. For the sake of my temper I hope your purpose in interrupting me is an excellent one.

"First, before you ask," Dallben went on, "I assure you the Princess Eilonwy is well and no more unhappy than any pretty young madcap obliged to turn a hand to sewing instead of sword-play. Second, you are as aware as I am that Kaw has not yet returned. By now, I daresay he has borne my potion to Glew's cavern, and the giant-by-accident who troubled you so much on Mona will shrink to the small stature he once had. But you also know your crow for a rascal and one to linger wherever he finds sport. Finally, an Assistant Pig-Keeper should have tasks enough to busy himself outdoors. What, then, brings you here?"

"One thing only," Taran said. "All that I have I owe to your kindness. You have given me a home and a name, and let me live as a son in your household. Yet who am I, in truth? Who are my parents? You have taught me much, but kept this always from me."

"Since it has been always thus," Dallben replied, "why should it trouble you now?"

When Taran bowed his head and did not answer, the old enchanter smiled shrewdly at him. "Speak up, my boy. If you want truth, you should begin by giving it. Behind your question I think I see the shadow of a certain golden-haired Princess. Is that not so?"

Taran's face flushed. "It is so," he murmured. He raised his eyes to meet Dallben's. "When Eilonwy returns, it—it is in my heart to ask her to wed. But this I cannot do," he burst out, "this I will not do until I learn who I am. An unknown foundling with a borrowed name cannot ask for the hand of a Princess. What is my parentage? I cannot rest until I know. Am I lowly born or nobly?"

"To my mind," Dallben said softly, "the latter would please you better."

"It would be my hope," Taran admitted, a little abashed. "But no matter. If there is honor—yes, let me share it. If there is shame, let me face it."

"It takes as much strength of heart to share the one as to face the other," Dallben replied gently. He turned his careworn face to Taran. "But alas," he said, "what you ask I may not answer. Prince Gwydion knows no more than I," he went on, sensing Taran's thought. "Nor can the High King Math help you."

"Then let me learn for myself," Taran cried. "Give me leave to seek my own answer."

Dallben studied him carefully. The enchanter's eyes fell on *The Book of Three* and he gazed long at it, as though his glance penetrated deep into the worn leather volume.

"Once the apple is ripe," he murmured to himself, "no man can turn it back to a greening." His voice grew heavy with sorrow as he said to Taran, "Is this indeed your wish?"

Taran's heart quickened. "I ask nothing more."

Dallben nodded. "So it must be. Journey, then, wherever you choose. Learn what lies in your power to learn."

"You have all my thanks," Taran cried joyfully, bowing deeply. "Let me start without delay. I am ready . . ."

Before he could finish the door burst open and a shaggy figure sped across the chamber and flung itself at Taran's feet. "No, no, no!" howled Gurgi at the top of his voice, rocking back and forth and waving his hairy arms. "Sharp-eared Gurgi hears all! Oh, yes, with listenings behind the door!" His face wrinkled in misery and he shook his matted head so violently he nearly sprawled flat on the floor. "Poor Gurgi will be lone and lorn with whinings and pinings!" he moaned. "Oh, he must go with master, yes, yes!"

Taran put a hand on Gurgi's shoulder. "It would sadden me to leave you, old friend. But my road, I fear, may be a long one."

"Faithful Gurgi will follow!" pleaded Gurgi. "He is strong, bold, and clever to keep kindly master from harmful hurtings!"

Gurgi began snuffling loudly, whimpering and moaning more desperately than before; and Taran, who could not bring himself to deny the unhappy creature, looked questioningly at Dallben.

A strange glance of pity crossed the enchanter's face. "Gurgi's staunchness and good sense I do not doubt," he said to Taran. "Though before your search is ended, the comfort of his kindly heart may stand you in better stead. Yes," he added slowly, "if Gurgi is willing, let him journey with you."

Gurgi gave a joyous yelp, and Taran bowed gratefully to the enchanter.

"So be it," Dallben said. "Your road indeed will not be easy, but set out on it as you choose. Though you may not find what you seek, you will surely return a little wiser—and perhaps even grown to manhood in your own right."

That night Taran lay restless. Dallben had agreed the two companions could depart in the morning, but for Taran the hours until sunrise weighed like the links of a heavy chain. A plan had formed in his mind, but he had said nothing of it to Dallben, Coll, or Gurgi; for he was half fearful of what he had decided. While his heart ached at the thought of leaving Caer Dallben, it ached the more with impatience to begin his journey; and it was as though his yearning for Eilonwy, the love he had often hidden or even denied, now swelled like a flood, driving him before it.

Long before dawn Taran rose and saddled the gray, silver-maned stallion, Melynlas. While Gurgi, blinking and yawning, readied his own mount, a short, stocky pony almost as shaggy as himself, Taran went alone to Hen Wen's enclosure. As though she had already sensed Taran's decision, the white pig squealed dolefully as he knelt and put an arm around her.

"Farewell, Hen," Taran said, scratching her bristly chin. "Remember me kindly. Coll will care for you until I . . . Oh, Hen," he murmured, "shall I come happily to the end of my quest? Can you tell me? Can you give me some sign of good hope?"

In answer, however, the oracular pig only wheezed and grunted anxiously. Taran sighed and gave Hen Wen a last affectionate pat. Dallben had hobbled into the dooryard, and beside him Coll raised a torch, for the morning still was dark. Like Dallben's, the old warrior's face in the wavering light was filled 15 with fond concern. Taran embraced them, and to him it seemed his love for both had never been greater than at this leave-taking as they said their farewells.

Gurgi sat hunched atop the pony. Slung from his shoulder was his leather wallet with its inexhaustible supply of food. Bearing only his sword at his belt and the silver-bound battle horn Eilonwy had given him, Taran swung astride the impatient Melynlas, constraining himself not to glance backward, knowing if he did, his parting would grieve him the more deeply.

The two wayfarers rode steadily while the sun climbed higher above the rolling, tree-fringed hills. Taran had spoken little, and Gurgi trotted quietly behind him, delving now and again into the leather wallet for a handful of food which he munched contentedly. When they halted to water their mounts at a stream, Gurgi clambered down and went to Taran's side.

"Kindly master," he cried, "faithful Gurgi follows as he leads, oh, yes! Where does he journey first with amblings and ramblings? To noble Lord Gwydion at Caer Dathyl? Gurgi longs to see high golden towers and great halls for feastings."

"I, too," answered Taran. "But it would be labor lost. Dallben has told me Prince Gwydion and King Math know nothing of my parentage."

"Then to kingdom of Fflewddur Fflam? Yes,

yes! Bold bard will welcome us with meetings and greetings, with merry hummings and strummings!"

Taran smiled at Gurgi's eagerness, but shook his head. "No, my friend, not to Caer Dathyl, nor to Fflewddur's realm." He turned his eyes westward. "I have thought carefully of this, and believe there is only one place where I might find what I seek," he said slowly. "The Marshes of Morva."

No sooner had he spoken these words than he saw Gurgi's face turn ashen. The creature's jaw dropped; he clapped his hands to his shaggy head, and began gasping and choking frightfully.

"No, oh, no!" Gurgi howled. "Dangers lurk in evil Marshes! Bold but cautious Gurgi fears for his poor tender head! He wants never to return there. Fearsome enchantresses would have turned him into a toad with hoppings and floppings! Oh, terrible Orddu! Terrible Orwen! And Orgoch, oh, Orgoch, worst of all!"

"Yet I mean to face them again," Taran said. "Orddu, Orwen, and Orgoch—she, or they, or whatever they may really be—are as powerful as Dallben. Perhaps more powerful. Nothing is hidden from them; all secrets are open. They would know the truth. Could it not be," he went on, his voice quickening hopefully, "could it not be that my parents were of noble lineage? And for some secret reason left me with Dallben to foster?"

17

"But kindly master *is* noble!" Gurgi cried. "Noble, generous, and good to humble Gurgi! No need to ask enchantresses!"

"I speak of noble blood," Taran replied, smiling at Gurgi's protests. "If Dallben cannot tell me, then Orddu may. Whether she will, I do not know," he added. "But I must try.

"I won't have you risk your poor tender head," Taran continued. "You shall find a hiding place at the edge of the Marshes and wait for me there."

"No, no," Gurgi moaned. He blinked wretchedly and his voice fell so low that Taran could scarcely hear his trembling whisper. "Faithful Gurgi follows, as he promised."

They set out again. For some days after fording Great Avren they bore quickly westward along the green slopes of the riverbank, leaving it reluctantly to wend north across a fallow plain. Gurgi's face puckered anxiously, and Taran sensed the creature's disquiet no less than his own. The closer they drew to the Marshes the more he questioned the wisdom of his choice. His plan which had seemed so fitting in the safety of Caer Dallben now struck him as rash, a foolhardy venture. There were moments when, Taran admitted to himself, had Gurgi spun the pony about and bolted homeward, he would have gladly done likewise.

Another day's travel and the marshland

stretched before them, bleak, ugly, untouched by spring. The sight and scent of the bogs and the dull, stagnant pools filled Taran with loathing. The rotting turf sucked greedily at the hooves of Melynlas. The pony snorted fearfully. Warning Gurgi to stay close behind him and stray neither to the right nor left, Taran cautiously guided the stallion through beds of reeds shoulder-high, keeping to the firmer ground at the rim of the swamps.

The narrow neck at the upper reaches of the Marshes could be crossed with least danger, and the path indeed was burned into his memory. Here, when he and Eilonwy, Gurgi, and Fflewddur had sought the Black Cauldron, the Huntsmen of Annuvin had attacked them, and Taran had lived the moment again and again in nightmares. Giving Melynlas rein, he beckoned to Gurgi and rode into the Marshes. The stallion faltered a sickening instant, then found footing on the chain of islands that lay beneath the brackish water. At the far side, without Taran's urging, Melynlas broke into a gallop, and the pony pelted after, as though fleeing for its life. Beyond the stunted trees at the end of a long gully, Taran halted. Orddu's cottage lay straight ahead.

Built against the side of a high mound, half-hidden by sod and branches, it seemed in even greater disrepair than Taran had remembered. The thatched roof, like a huge bird's nest, straggled down to block the narrow windows; a spider web of mold covered the walls, which looked ready to tumble at any moment. In the crooked doorway stood Orddu herself.

Heart pounding, Taran swung from the saddle. Holding his head high, in a silence broken only by the chattering of Gurgi's teeth, he strode slowly across the dooryard. Orddu was watching him with sharp, black eyes. If she was surprised, the enchantress gave no sign other than to bend forward a little and peer more closely at Taran. Her shapeless robe flapped about her knees; the jeweled clasps and pins glittered in her weedy tangle of disheveled hair as she nodded her head rapidly and with evident satisfaction.

"Yes, and so it is!" Orddu called out pleasantly. "The dear little fledgling and the—whatever-you-call-it. But you've grown much taller, my duck. How troublesome it must be should you ever want to climb down a rabbit hole. Come in, come in," she hurried on, beckoning. "So pale you are, poor thing. You've not been ill?"

Taran followed her not without uneasiness, while Gurgi, shuddering, clung to him. "Beware, beware," the creature whimpered. "Warm welcomings give Gurgi frosty chillings."

The three enchantresses, so far as Taran could see, had been busy at household tasks. Orgoch, her black hood shrouding her features, sat on a rickety stool, trying without great success to tease cockleburs from a lapful of wool shearings. Orwen, if indeed it was Orwen, was turning a rather lopsided spinning wheel; the milky white beads dangling from her neck seemed in danger of catching in the spokes. Orddu herself, he guessed, had been at the loom that stood amid piles of ancient, rusted weapons in a corner of the cottage. The work on the frame had gone forward somewhat, but it was far from done; knotted, twisted threads straggled in all directions, and what looked like some of Orgoch's cockleburs were snagged in the warp and weft. Taran could make out nothing of the pattern, though it seemed to him, as if by some trick of his eyes, that vague shapes, human and animal, moved and shifted through the weaving.

But he had no chance to study the curious tapestry. Orwen, leaving the wheel, hastened to him, clapping her hands delightedly.

"The wandering chicken and the gurgi!" she cried. "And how is dear little Dallben? Does he still have *The Book of Three*? And his beard? How heavy it must be for him. The book, not the beard," she added. "Did he not come with you? More's the pity. But no matter. It's so charming to have visitors."

"I don't care for visitors," muttered Orgoch, irritably tossing the wool to the ground. "They disagree with me."

"Of course they do, greedy thing!" Orwen replied sharply. "And a wonder it is that we have any at all."

At this, Orgoch snorted and mumbled under her breath. Beneath her black hood Taran glimpsed a shadowy grimace.

Orddu raised a hand. "Pay Orgoch no heed," she said to Taran. "She's out of sorts today, poor dear. It was Orwen's turn to be Orgoch, and Orgoch was so looking forward to being Orwen. Now she's disappointed, since Orwen at the last moment simply refused—not that I blame her," Orddu whispered. "I don't enjoy being Orgoch either. But we'll make it up to her somehow.

"And you," Orddu went on, a smile wrinkling her lumpy face, "you are the boldest of bold goslings. Few in Prydain have been willing to brave the Marshes of Morva; and of those few, not one has dared to return. Perhaps Orgoch disheartens them. You alone have done so, my chick."

"Oh, Orddu, he is a brave hero," Orwen put in, looking at Taran with girlish admiration.

"Don't talk nonsense, Orwen," Orddu replied. "There are heroes and heroes. I don't deny he's acted bravely on occasion. He's fought beside Lord Gwydion and been proud of himself as a chick wearing eagle's feathers. But that's only one kind of bravery. Has the darling robin ever scratched for his own worms? That's bravery of another sort. And between the two, dear Orwen, he might find the latter shows the greater courage." The enchantress turned to Taran. "But speak up, my fledgling. Why do you seek us again?"

"Don't tell us," interrupted Orwen. "Let us guess. Oh, but I do love games, though Orgoch always spoils them." She giggled. "You shall give us a thousand and three guesses and I shall be first to ask."

"Very well, Orwen, if it pleases you," Orddu said indulgently. "But are a thousand and three enough? A young lamb can want for so much."

"Your concern is with things as they are," Taran said, forcing himself to look the enchantress in the eyes, "and with things as they must be. I believe you know my quest from its beginning to its end, and that I seek to learn my parentage."

"Parentage?" said Orddu. "Nothing easier. Choose any parents you please. Since none of you has ever known each other, what difference can it possibly make—to them or to you? Believe what you like. You'll be surprised how comforting it is."

"I ask no comfort," Taran replied, "but the truth, be it harsh or happy."

"Ah, my sweet robin," said Orddu, "for the finding of that, nothing is harder. There are those who have spent lifetimes at it, and many in worse plight than yours.

"There was a frog, some time ago," Orddu

went on cheerfully. "I remember him well, poor dear; never sure whether he was a land creature, who liked swimming under water, or a water creature, who liked sunning himself on logs. We turned him into a stork with a keen appetite for frogs, and from then on he had no doubts as to who he was—nor did the other frogs, for the matter of that. We would gladly do the same for you."

"For both of you," said Orgoch.

"No!" yelled Gurgi, ducking behind Taran. "Oh, kindly master, Gurgi warned of fearsome changings and arrangings!"

"Don't forget the serpent," Orwen told Orddu, "all fretted and perplexed because he didn't know if he was green with brown spots or brown with green ones. We made him an invisible serpent," she added, "with brown and green spots, so he could be clearly seen and not trodden on. He was so grateful and much easier in his mind after that."

"And I recall," croaked Orgoch, huskily clearing her throat, "there was a . . ."

"Do be still, Orgoch," Orwen interrupted. "Your tales always have such—such untidy endings."

"You see, my pullet," Orddu said, "we can help you in many ways, all quicker and simpler than any you might think of. What would you rather be? If you want my opinion, I suggest a hedgehog; it's a safer life than most. But don't let me sway your choice; it's entirely up to you."

"On the contrary, let's surprise them," cried Orwen in happy excitement. "We'll decide among ourselves and spare them the tedious business of making up their minds. They'll be all the more pleased. How charming it will be to see the look on their little faces—or beaks or whatever it is they finally have."

"No fowls," grumbled Orgoch. "No fowls, in any case. Can't abide them. Feathers make me cough."

Gurgi's fright had so mounted he could only babble wordlessly. Taran felt his own blood run cold. Orddu had taken a step forward and Taran defensively reached for his sword.

"Now, now, my chicken," Orddu cheerily remarked, "don't lose your temper, or you may lose considerably more. You know your blade is useless here, and waving swords is no way to set anyone in a proper frame of mind. It was you who chose to put yourselves in our hands."

"Hands?" growled Orgoch. From the depths of the hood her eyes flashed redly and her mouth began twitching.

Taran stood firm. "Orddu," he said, keeping his voice as steady as he could, "will you tell me what I ask? If not, we will go our way."

"We were only trying to make things easier for you," said Orwen, pouting and fingering her beads. "You needn't take offense."

"Of course we shall tell you, my brave tadpole," Orddu said. "You shall know all you seek to know, directly we've settled another matter: the price to be paid. Since what you ask is of such importance —to yourself, at least—the cost may be rather high. But I'm sure you thought of that before you came."

"When we sought the Black Cauldron," Taran began, "you took Adaon's enchanted brooch in fee, the one thing I treasured most. Since then I have found nothing I have prized more."

"But, my chicken," said Orddu, "we struck that bargain long ago; it is over and done. Are you saying you brought nothing with you? Why, count yourself lucky to become a hedgehog, since you can afford little else."

"Last time," Orgoch hoarsely whispered in Orddu's ear, "you would have taken one of the young lamb's summer days, and a tasty morsel it would have been."

"You are always thinking of your own pleasures, Orgoch," replied Orddu. "You might at least try to think of what we all would like."

"There was a golden-haired girl with him then," Orwen put in, "a pretty little creature. He surely has lovely memories of her. Could we not take them?" She went on eagerly. "How delightful it would be to spread them out and look at them during long winter evenings. Alas, he would have none for himself, but I think it would be an excellent bargain."

Taran caught his breath. "Even you would not be so pitiless."

"Would we not?" answered Orddu, smiling. "Pity, dear gosling—as you know it, at least—simply doesn't enter into the question as far as we're concerned. However," she went on, turning to Orwen, "that won't answer either. We already have quite enough memories."

"Hear me then," cried Taran, drawing himself to his full height. He clenched his hands to keep them from trembling. "It is true I own little to treasure, not even my name. Is there nothing you will have of me? This I offer you," he went on quickly in a low voice. He felt his brow dampen. Though he had taken this decision at Caer Dallben and weighed it carefully, with the moment upon him, he nearly faltered and longed to turn from it.

"Whatever thing of value I may find in all my life to come," Taran said, "the greatest treasure that may come into my hands—I pledge it to you now. It shall be yours, and you shall claim it when you please."

Orddu did not answer, only looked at him

curiously. The other enchantresses were silent. Even Gurgi had ceased his whimpering. The shapes on the loom seemed to writhe before Taran's eyes as he waited for Orddu to speak.

The enchantress smiled. "Does your quest mean so much that you will spend what you have not yet gained?"

"Or may never gain," croaked Orgoch.

"No more can I offer," Taran cried. "You cannot refuse me."

"The kind of bargain you propose," said Orddu in a pleasant but matter-of-fact tone, "is a chancy thing at best, and really satisfies no one. Nothing is all that certain, and very often we've found the poor sparrow who makes such a pledge never lives long enough to fulfill it. When he does, there is always the risk of his turning—well, shall we say—a little stubborn? It usually ends with unhappy feelings all around. Once, we might have accepted. But sad experience made us put a stop to it altogether. No, my fledgling, it won't do. We're sorry; that is, sorry as much as we can feel sorrow for anything."

Taran's voice caught in his throat. For an instant the features of the enchantress shifted; he could not be sure whether it was Orddu, Orwen, or Orgoch whom he faced. It was as though there had risen in front of him a wall of ice which force could not breach nor pleading melt. Despair choked him. He bowed his head and turned away.

"But my dear gosling," Orddu called cheerily, "that's not to say there aren't others to answer your question."

"Of course there are," added Orwen, "and the finding takes no more than the looking."

"Who, then?" Taran asked urgently, seizing on this new hope.

"I recall a brown-and-orange ousel that comes once a year to sharpen his beak on Mount Kilgwyry," said Orwen. "He knows all that has ever happened. If you're patient you might wait and ask him."

"Oh, Orwen," Orddu interrupted with some impatience, "sometimes I do believe you dwell too much in the past. Mount Kilgwyry has been worn down long ago with his pecking and the little darling has flown elsewhere."

"You're so right, dear Orddu," replied Orwen. "It had slipped my mind for a moment. But what of the salmon of Lake Llew? I've never met a wiser fish."

"Gone," muttered Orgoch, sucking a tooth. "Long gone."

"In any case, ousels and fishes are flighty and slippery," Orddu said. "Something more reliable would serve better. You might, for example, try the Mirror of Llunet."

"The Mirror of Llunet?" Taran repeated. "I have never heard it spoken of. What is it? Where . . ."

"Best yet," Orgoch broke in, "he could stay with us. And the gurgi, too."

"Do try to control yourself, dear Orgoch, when I'm explaining something," Orddu remarked, then turned back to Taran. "Yes, perhaps if you looked into it, the Mirror of Llunet would show you something of interest."

"But where," Taran began again.

"Too far," grumbled Orgoch. "Stay, by all means."

"In the Llawgadarn Mountains," replied Orddu, taking him by the arm, "if it hasn't been moved. But come along, my gosling. Orgoch is growing restless. I know she'd enjoy having you here, and with two disappointments in the same day I shouldn't want to account for her behavior."

"But how may I find it?" Taran could do no more than stammer his question before he was outside the cottage, with Gurgi trembling at his side.

"Don't tarry in the Marshes," Orddu called, while from within the cottage Taran heard loud and angry noises. "Else you may regret your foolish boldness—or bold foolishness, whichever. Farewell, my robin."

The crooked door closed tightly, even as Taran cried out for Orddu to wait.

"Flee!" Gurgi yelped. "Flee, kindly master, while Gurgi's poor tender head is still on his shoulders!"

Despite the creature's frantic tugging at his arm, Taran stood staring at the door. His thoughts were confused, a strange heaviness had settled upon him.

"Why did she mock my bravery?" he said, frowning. "Courage to scratch for worms? That task would be far easier than seeking the Mirror of Llunet."

"Hasten!" Gurgi pleaded. "Gurgi has his fill of questings. Now he is ready for returnings to safe and happy Caer Dallben, yes, yes! Oh, do not make useless peekings and seekings!"

Taran hesitated a moment longer. Of the Llawgadarn Mountains he knew only that they rose far to the east. With nothing to guide his search the journey might indeed prove useless. Gurgi looked imploringly at him. Taran patted the creature's shoulder, then turned and strode to Melynlas.

"The Mirror of Llunet is the only hope Orddu has given me," Taran said. "I must find it."

While Gurgi hastily mounted his pony, Taran swung astride Melynlas. He glanced once again at the cottage, his heart suddenly uneasy. "Given me?" he murmured. "Does Orddu give anything for nothing?"

CHAPTER II

Cantrev Cadiffor

The two companions left the Marshes of Morva, pressing southeastward to the Valley Cantrevs along the Ystrad River, for Taran had decided to break his journey at Caer Cadarn, fortress of King Smoit, and ask the red-bearded King to refit them with gear sturdier than what they had brought from Caer Dallben. "From there," Taran told Gurgi, "we can only search as the moment guides us. My poor tender head is full of questions," he sighed, with a wry and regretful smile, "but of plans, alas, none at all."

With the Marshes many days behind, the two companions crossed the borders of Cadiffor, Smoit's realm and largest of the Valley Cantrevs. The countryside had long since changed from gray moors to green meadows and pleasantly wooded lands with farmholds nestled in the clearings. Though Gurgi eyed the dells longingly, sniffing the smoke of cookfires wafting from the cottage chimneys, Taran did not turn from the path he had chosen. By keeping a brisk pace, another three days of travel would bring them to Caer Cadarn. A little before sundown, seeing the clouds growing heavy and dark, Taran halted to find shelter in a pine grove.

He had scarcely dismounted, and Gurgi had only begun to unlash the saddlebags, when a band of horsemen cantered into the grove. Taran spun around and drew his blade. Gurgi, yelping in alarm, scurried to his master's side.

There were five riders, well-mounted and armed, their rough-bearded faces sun-blackened, their bearing that of men long used to the saddle. The colors they wore were not those of the House of Smoit, and Taran guessed the horsemen to be warriors in the service of one of Smoit's liegemen.

"Put up your blade," commanded the leading rider, nevertheless drawing his own, reining up before the wayfarers and glancing scornfully at them. "Who are you? Who do you serve?"

"They're outlaws," cried another. "Strike them down."

"They look more like scarecrows than outlaws," replied the leader. "I take them for a pair of churls who have run away from their master."

Taran lowered his sword but did not sheathe it. "I am Taran Assistant Pig-Keeper . . ."

"Where then are your pigs?" cried the first rider with a coarse laugh. "And why are you not at 33 keeping them?" He gestured with a thumb toward Gurgi. "Or will you tell me this—this sorry thing is one of your charges?"

"He is no piggy!" indignantly retorted Gurgi. "No piggy at all! He is Gurgi, bold and clever to serve kindly master!"

The creature's outburst brought only more laughter from the horsemen. But now the first rider spied Melynlas. "Your steed is above your station, pig-keeper," he said. "How do you come by it?"

"Melynlas is mine by right," Taran replied sharply. "A gift of Gwydion Prince of Don."

"Lord Gwydion?" cried the warrior. "Given? Stolen from him, rather," he jeered. "Have a care; your lies will cost you a beating."

"I tell no lie and seek no quarrel," Taran answered. "We journey in peace to King Smoit's castle."

"Smoit needs no pig-keeper," one of the warriors broke in.

"Nor do we," said the first rider. He swung around to his fellows. "What say you? Shall we take his horse or his head? Or both?"

"Lord Goryon will welcome a fresh mount and reward us all the more for this one," answered a rider. "But the head of a pig-keeper serves no use, not even to himself."

"Well said, and so be it!" cried the warrior. "Besides, he can better mind his pigs afoot," he added, reaching for the stallion's bridle.

Taran sprang between Melynlas and the horse-man. Gurgi leaped forward and furiously grappled the rider's leg. The other warriors spurred their mounts, and Taran found himself in the midst of rearing horses, driven from the side of his own steed. He fought to bring up his sword. One of the riders wheeled and drove his mount's flank heavily against Taran, who lost his footing. At the same instant another of his assailants fetched him a blow that would surely have cost Taran his head had the warrior not struck with the flat of his sword. As it was, Taran fell stunned to the ground, his ears ringing, thoughts spinning, and the horsemen seeming to burst into comets before his eyes. He was dimly aware of Gurgi frantically yelling, of Melynlas whinnying, and it seemed to him that another figure had joined the fray. By the time he could stagger to his feet, the horsemen had vanished, dragging Melynlas with them.

Taran, crying out in dismay and anger, stumbled toward the path they had taken. A broad hand grasped his shoulder. He turned abruptly to see a man in a sleeveless jacket of coarse wool girt with a plaited rope. His bare arms were knotted and sinewy, and his back bent, though less by years than by labor. A shock of gray, uncropped hair hung about a face that was stern but not unkind.

"Hold, hold," the man said. "You'll not overtake them now. Your horse will come to no ill. The henchmen of Lord Goryon treat steeds better than strangers." He patted the oaken staff he carried. "Two of Goryon's border-band will have heads to mend. But so will you, from the look of you." He picked up a sack and slung it over his shoulder. "I am Aeddan Son of Aedd," he said. "Come, both of you. My farm is no distance."

"Without Melynlas my quest will fail," Taran cried. "I must find—" He stopped short. The warriors' mockery still rankled him, and he was reluctant to tell more than need be, even to this man who had befriended him.

But the farmer showed no interest in questioning him. "What you seek," replied Aeddan, "is more your business than mine. I saw five set upon two and only put some fairness in the match. Will you heal your hurt? Then follow me."

So saying, the farmer set off down the hillside, Taran and Gurgi behind him. Gurgi turned often to shake his fist in the direction of the departed horsemen, while Taran trudged along the darkening path, speaking not a word, deep in despair over Melynlas, and thinking bitterly that in his quest he had done no more than lose his horse and gain a broken head. His bones ached; his muscles throbbed. To worsen matters, the clouds had thickened; nightfall brought a pelting rain; and by the time he reached Aeddan's farmhold Taran was as drenched and bedraggled as ever he had been in all his life.

The dwelling into which Aeddan led the companions was only a hut of wattle and daub, but Taran was surprised at its snugness and neat furnishings. Never before in all his adventures had he shared hospitality with the farmer folk of Prydain, and he glanced around as wondering as a stranger in a new land. Now that he could look more closely at Aeddan, he sensed honesty and good nature in the man's weathered face. The farmer gave him a warm grin and Taran, despite the smart of his wounds, grinned back, feeling indeed that he had come upon a friend.

The farm wife, a tall, work-hardened woman with features as lined as her husband's, threw up her hands at the sight of Gurgi, whose dripping, matted hair had gathered a blanket of twigs and pine needles, and cried out at Taran's blood-smeared face. While Aeddan told of the fray, the woman, Alarca, opened a wooden chest and drew out a sturdy, warm jacket, well worn but lovingly mended, which Taran gratefully took in place of his own sodden garment.

Alarca set about mixing a potion of healing herbs, and Aeddan, meantime, poured onto a table the contents of his sack: hunches of bread, a cheese, and some dried fruit.

37

"You come to small comfort," he said. "My land yields little, so I toil part of my days in my neighbors' fields to earn what I cannot grow."

"And yet," Taran said, dismayed to learn Aeddan's plight, "I have heard it told there was rich soil in the Valley Cantrevs."

"Was, indeed," replied Aeddan with a dour laugh. "In the time of my forefathers, not in mine. As the Hill Cantrevs were famed for their long-fleeced sheep, so the Valley Cantrevs of Ystrad were known far and wide for the finest oats and barley, and Cantrev Cadiffor itself for wheat bright and heavy as gold. And golden days there must have been in all Prydain," Aeddan went on, cutting the bread and cheese into portions and handing them to Taran and Gurgi. "My father's father told a tale, already old when it was told to him, of plows that worked of themselves, of scythes that reaped a harvest without even the touch of a man's hand."

"So, too, have I heard," Taran said. "But Arawn Death-Lord stole those treasures, and now they lie unused and hidden deep in the fastness of Annuvin."

The farmer nodded. "Arawn's hand chokes the life from Prydain. His shadow blights the land. Our toil grows heavier, and all the more because our skills are few. Enchanted tools did Arawn steal? Many secrets there were of making the earth yield richly, and of these, too, the Lord of Annuvin robbed us.

"Twice in two years have my crops failed," Aeddan went on, as Taran listened with heartfelt concern. "My granary is empty. And the more I must toil for others, the less I may work my own fields. Even so, my knowledge is too slight. What I most need is locked forever in the treasure hoard of Annuvin."

"It is not altogether your skill that lacks," Alarca said, putting a hand on the farmer's knotted shoulder. "Before the first planting the plow ox and cow sickened and died. And the second," her voice lowered. "For the second we were without the help of Amren."

Taran glanced questioningly at the woman, whose eyes had clouded.

She said, "Amren, our son. He was of your years, and it is his jacket you wear. He needs it no longer. Winter and summer are alike to him. He sleeps under a burial mound among other fallen warriors. Yes, he is gone," the woman added. "He rode with the battle host when they fought off raiders who sought to plunder us."

"I share your sorrow," Taran said; then, to console her, added, "But he died with honor. Your son is a hero . . ."

"My son is slain," the woman answered sharply. "The raiders fought because they were starving; we, because we had scarcely more than they. And at the end all had less than when they began. Now, for us the labor is too great for one pair of hands, even for two. The secrets Arawn Death-Lord stole could well serve us. Alas, we cannot regain them."

"No matter. Even without the secrets my harvest will not fail this year," Aeddan said. "All save one of my fields lies fallow; but in this one have I spent all my toil." He looked proudly at Taran. "When my wife and I could no longer pull the plow ourselves, I broke the earth with my own hands and sowed it grain by grain." The farmer laughed. "Yes, and weeded it blade by blade, as niggling as a granddam with her favorite patch of herbs. It will not fail. Indeed, it must not," he added, frowning. "This season our livelihood hangs on it."

Little more was said then, and when the meager meal ended, Taran gladly stretched his aching bones besides the hearth, while Gurgi curled up next to him. Weariness overcame even his despair for Melynlas, and with the patter of rain on the thatch and the hiss of the dying embers Taran soon fell asleep.

The companions woke before first light, but

Taran found Aeddan already working in his field. The rain had stopped, leaving the earth fresh and moist. Taran knelt and took up a handful. Aeddan had spoken the truth. The soil had been tilled with utmost pains, and Taran watched the farmer with growing respect and admiration. The farm could indeed yield richly, and Taran stood a moment looking toward the fallow ground, barren for lack of hands to labor it. With a sigh he turned quickly away, his thoughts once more on Melynlas.

How he might regain the silver-maned stallion Taran could not foresee, but he had determined to make his way to the stronghold of Lord Goryon where, in Aeddan's judgment, the warriors had surely taken the animal. Though more than ever anxious over his beloved steed, Taran worked through the morning beside Aeddan. The farm couple had kept scarcely a morsel of the evening's fare for themselves, and Taran saw no other means to repay them. By midday, however, he dared delay no longer, and made ready to take his leave.

Alarca had come to the door of the hut. Like her husband, the woman had asked nothing beyond what little Taran had chosen to tell of his quest, but now she said, "Will you still follow your own path? Have you turned from home and kinsmen? What mother's heart longs for her son as I long for mine?" 41

"Alas, none that I know," Taran answered, folding Amren's jacket and gently putting it in her hands. "And none that knows me."

"You have been well taught in the ways of farming," Aeddan said. "If you seek a place of welcome, you have already found one."

"Whatever other welcomes I find, may they be as openhearted as yours," Taran replied, and it was not without regret that he and Gurgi said farewell.

CHAPTER III

Goryon and Gast

eddan had pointed out the shortest path to Lord Goryon's stronghold, and the two wayfarers reached it by midafternoon. It was not a castle, Taran saw, but a large huddle of buildings circled by a barricade of wooden stakes lashed with osier and chinked up with hard-packed earth. The gate of heavy palings stood open, and there was much going and coming of horsemen, of warriors on foot, of herdsmen driving in their cows from pasture.

Though Gurgi was far from eager, Taran led on, keeping as bold a face as he could, and amid the busy crowd the two entered the stronghold unnoticed and unchallenged. Without difficulty Taran found the stables, which were larger, cleaner, and in better repair than the rest of the buildings; and strode quickly to a young boy raking straw, calling out in a firm voice, "Tell me, friend, is there not a gray stallion here that Lord Goryon's warriors captured? A handsome steed, they say, and a rare one."

"Gray stallion?" cried the stable boy. "Gray dragon, rather! The beast half-kicked his stall down and gave me a bite I'll not forget. Lord Goryon will have broken bones before the day ends."

"How then?" Taran hurriedly asked. "What has he done with the steed?"

"What has the steed done with him!" answered the boy, grinning. "Thrown him the most of a dozen times already! The Master of Horse himself cannot sit three moments on the creature's back, but Goryon tries to ride it even now. Goryon the Valorous he is called," the boy chuckled; then added behind his hand, "though to my mind he has little stomach for this task. But his henchmen egg him on, and so Goryon means to break the beast to his will even if he must first break its back."

"Master, master," Gurgi whispered frantically, "hasten to King Smoit for helpings!"

Taran's face had paled at the boy's words. Caer Cadarn was too far; Smoit's help would come too late. "Where is the steed?" he asked, hiding his concern. "This would be a sight worth the seeing."

The stable boy pointed his rake toward a long, low-roofed building. "In the training field behind the Great Hall. But take heed," he added, rubbing his shoulder, "keep your distance, or the beast will give you worse than he gave me."

Setting off instantly Taran no sooner passed the Great Hall than he heard shouting and the furious whinny of Melynlas. His pace quickened into a run. A grassless, hoofbeaten turf was ahead. He glimpsed warriors circling the gray stallion who reared, bucked, and spun about with heels flying. In another moment the burly, thickset figure atop the stallion's back was flung loose; then, arms and legs flailing, Lord Goryon plummeted to earth and lay there like a sack of lead.

Melynlas galloped desperately, seeking escape from the circle of warriors, one of whom hastened to snatch at the horse's reins. All caution forgotten, Taran cried out and raced to the stallion's side. He grasped the bridle before the surprised man could think of drawing his sword, and threw his arms about the neck of Melynlas, who whickered in greeting. The other onlookers ran toward Taran, as he strove to mount and pull Gurgi up after him. A hand seized his jacket. Taran fought free and set his back against the stallion's flank. Lord Goryon had meanwhile picked himself up and now burst through the press of warriors.

"Insolence! Impudence!" roared Goryon. His dark, gray-shot beard bristled like a furious hedgehog. His heavy face was mottled purple, whether from bruises, lack of breath, blind anger, or all three 45 at once Taran could not judge. "Does a churl lay hand on my horse? Away with him! Thrash him soundly for his insult!"

"I do no more than claim my own steed," Taran cried. "Melynlas foal of Melyngar . . ."

A tall, raw-boned man with one arm bound up in a sling, whom Taran guessed to be the Master of Horse, peered sharply at him. "Foal of Melyngar, Prince Gwydion's war horse? That is noble lineage. How do you know this?"

"I know it as well as I know Melynlas was stolen from me," Taran declared, "near Aeddan's farmhold at the borders of your cantrev, and my comrade robbed of his pony." He tried then to explain who he was and the purpose of his journey, but the cantrev lord, unheeding, broke in angrily.

"Impudence!" cried Goryon, his beard bristling all the more furiously. "How dares a pig-keeper insult me with a liar's tale? My border-band gained these mounts nearly at the cost of their lives."

"The cost of *our* lives," Taran retorted, glancing hurriedly at the faces around him. "Where are the riders? I beg you call them to witness."

"More insolence!" snapped the cantrev lord. "They ride the borders, as they are commanded. Do you mean to tell me I keep idle men and shirkers in my service?"

"And full service have they given you," one of

the warriors said to Goryon. "Heroes, all of them, to stand against six giants . . ."

"Giants?" repeated Taran, scarcely believing his ears.

"Giants indeed!" cried Goryon. "It will not be forgotten how the brave riders of Goryon the Valorous were beset by enemies, outnumbered two to one. By worse than giants! For one was a fierce monster with sharp claws and fangs. Another carried an oak tree in his fist and swept it about him as if it were no more than a twig. But the riders of Goryon overcame them all with glory and honor!"

"The stallion, too, was bewitched," put in another of Goryon's henchmen, "and fought as fiercely as the giants. The beast is a man-killer, vicious as a starving wolf."

"But Goryon the Valorous will tame the creature," added another, turning to the cantrev lord. "You'll ride the brute, will you not, Goryon?"

"Eh?" said Goryon, a painful and unhappy grimace suddenly marking his face. "So I will, so I will," he growled; then flung out angrily, "You insult my honor if you think I cannot."

As Taran stood among these rough warriors, he began to despair of finding any means of convincing the prickly-tempered cantrev lord; the thought crossed his mind to draw blade and fight his way out as best he could. But another glance at the stern faces of the henchmen gave him only more cause for dismay.

"My lord," Taran said firmly, "I speak the truth. There were no giants, but my companion and myself, and a farmer who fought beside us."

"No giants?" shouted Goryon. "But more insults!" He stamped his foot as if the turf itself had given him some impertinence. "You call my men liars? As well call me one!"

"My lord," Taran began again, bowing deeply, for it was growing clear to him that Goryon's touchy honor could scarcely allow the cantrev lord to believe an account of simple horse-stealing; and there was, Taran realized, even for the border-band themselves, considerably more honor in overcoming giants than in robbing Assistant Pig-Keepers. "I call no man liar and your men spoke the truth. The truth," he added, "as they saw it."

"Insolence!" cried Goryon. "The truth as it is! There were giants, monsters, uprooted oaks. My men were well-rewarded for their valor, but you shall have a beating for your impudence!"

"What I believe, my lord, is this," Taran went on, choosing his words carefully, since all he had thus far managed to say Goryon had turned into one kind of insult or another. "The sun was low and our shadows made our number seem twice as great. Indeed, your men saw double what we truly were.

"As for giants," Taran hurried on before the cantrev lord could cry out against another impertinence, "again, the long shadows of sunset gave us such height that any man could mistake our size."

"The oak-tree cudgel," Lord Goryon began.

"The farmer bore a stout oaken staff," Taran said. "His arm was strong, his blows quick, as two of your men had good reason to know. He smote with such a mighty hand, small wonder they felt a tree had fallen on them."

Lord Goryon said nothing for a moment, but sucked a tooth and rubbed his bristling beard. "What of the monster? A raving, ferocious creature they saw with their own eyes?"

"The monster stands before you," Taran answered, pointing to Gurgi. "He has long been my companion. I know him to be gentle, but the fiercest foe when roused."

"He is Gurgi! Yes, yes!" Gurgi shouted. "Bold, clever, and fierce to fight for kindly master!" With this he bared his teeth, shook his hairy arms, and yelled so frightfully that Goryon and his henchmen drew backward a pace.

The face of the cantrev lord had begun to furrow in deep perplexity. He shifted his bulk from one foot to another and glared at Taran. "Shadows!" he growled. "You mean to shadow the bravery of those who serve me. Another insult . . ."

"If your warriors believed they had seen what they claimed," Taran said, "and fought accordingly, their bravery is no less. Indeed," he added, half under his breath, "it is every bit as great as their truthfulness."

"These are no more than words," interrupted the Master of Horse. "Show me deeds. There is no creature on four hooves that I cannot ride, save this one. You, churl, will you dare to mount?"

For answer, Taran swung quickly into the saddle. Melynlas whinnied, pawed the ground, then stood calmly. Lord Goryon choked with amazement, and the Master of Horse stared in disbelief. A surprised murmur rose from Goryon's henchmen, but Taran heard a rough laugh as one of them called, "So ho, Goryon! A lout rides a steed a lord has not mastered, and takes your horse and honor both!"

Taran thought he had seen a faint flicker of relief in Goryon's bruised face, as though he were not altogether displeased to avoid riding Melynlas, but at the henchman's words the cantrev lord's features began to darken furiously.

"Not so!" Taran hastily cried out to the circle of men. "Would you have your liege lord ride a pig-keeper's nag? Is that fitting to his honor?" He turned now to Goryon, for a bold thought had come to him. "And yet, my lord, were you to take him as a gift from me . . ."

"What?" shouted Goryon at the top of his voice, his face turning livid. "Insults! Impertinence! Insolence! How dare you! I take no gifts from pig-keepers! Nor will I lower myself to mount the beast again." He flung up an arm. "Begone! Out of my sight —your nag, your monster, and his pony along with you!"

Goryon snapped his jaws shut and said no more. Gurgi's pony was led from the stable, and under the eyes of the cantrev lord and his henchmen the two companions passed unhindered through the gate.

Taran rode slowly, head high, with all the assurance he could muster. But once out of sight of the stronghold, the companions clapped heels into their horses' flanks and galloped for dear life.

"Oh, wisdom that wins horses from prideful lord!" Gurgi cried, when they had ridden far enough to be safe from any change of heart on the part of Goryon. "Even Gurgi could not have been so clever. Oh, he wishes to be wise as kindly master, but his poor tender head has no skill in such thinkings!"

"My wisdom?" Taran laughed. "Barely enough to make up for losing Melynlas in the first place." He scanned the valley anxiously. Night was falling and he had hoped by this time to have come upon a farmhold where they might shelter, for the encounter with Goryon's border-band had given him no wish to learn what others might be roving the hills. But he saw neither cottage nor hut, and so pressed on through the purpling dusk.

Lights flared in a clearing ahead, and Taran reined Melynlas to a halt near a stronghold much like Lord Goryon's. But here torches blazed at every corner of the palisade, from sockets set high on either side of the gate, even at the rooftree of the Great Hall, as if in token of feasting and revelry within.

"Dare we stop here?" Taran said. "If this cantrev lord shows us Goryon's courtesy, we'd sleep sounder in a gwythaint's nest." Nevertheless, the hope of a comfortable bed and the torches' inviting glow made his weariness weigh all the heavier. He hesitated a moment, then urged Melynlas closer to the gate.

To the men in the watchtower Taran called out that here were wayfarers journeying to Caer Cadarn and known to King Smoit. He was relieved when the portal creaked open and the guards beckoned the pair to enter. The Chief Steward was summoned, and he led Taran and Gurgi to the Great Hall.

"Beg hospitality of my Lord Gast," the Steward told them, "and he will grant what he deems

fitting."

As he followed the Steward, Taran's spirits rose at the thought of a warm meal and a comfortable couch. Loud voices, laughter, and the merry notes of a harp came from the Hall. Stepping through the doorway Taran saw crowded tables on either side of a low-ceilinged room. At the far end, flanked by his henchmen and their ladies, sat a richly garbed war lord, a drinking horn in one fist and most of a joint of meat in the other.

Taran and Gurgi bowed deeply. Before they could draw closer, the harper standing in the middle of the Hall turned, cried out in surprise, and ran to them. Taran, whose hand was being shaken half off his arm, found himself blinking with happy astonishment at the long pointed nose and spiky yellow hair of his old companion, Fflewddur Fflam.

"Well met, the two of you," cried the bard, pulling them to the high table. "I've missed you ever since we parted. Did you not stay at Caer Dallben? When we sailed from Mona," Fflewddur hurriedly explained, "I really meant to leave off wandering and settle down in my own realm. Then I said to myself, Fflewddur old fellow, spring's only once a year. And here it is. And here am I. But what of yourselves? First, food and drink, and your tidings later."

Fflewddur had brought the companions to stand before Lord Gast, and Taran saw a heavy-featured warrior with a beard the color of muddy 53 flax. A handsome collarpiece dangled from his neck; rings glittered on fingers stout enough to crack walnuts; and bands of beaten silver circled his arms. The cantrev lord's raiment was costly and well-cut, but Taran saw it bore the spots and spatters not only of this feast but of many others long past.

The bard, with a sweep of his harp, named the companions to Lord Gast. "These are two who sought the Black Cauldron from Arawn of Annuvin and fought at the side of Gwydion Prince of Don. Let your hospitality match their boldness."

"And so it shall!" Gast loudly cried. "No wayfarer can fault the hospitality of Gast the Generous!" He made place for the companions at his table and, sweeping aside the empty bowls and dishes before him, clapped his hands and bawled for the Steward. When the servitor arrived, Lord Gast commanded him to bring such an array of food and drink that Taran could hardly imagine himself eating half of it. Gurgi, hungry as always, smacked his lips in gleeful anticipation.

As the Steward left, Lord Gast took up a tale, whose matter Taran found difficult to follow, concerning the costliness of his food and his openhandedness toward travelers. Taran listened courteously through it all, surprised and delighted at his good luck in finding Gast's stronghold. Feeling more at ease, thanks to the presence of Fflewddur, Taran at last ventured to speak of his meeting with Lord Goryon.

"Goryon!" snorted Gast. "Arrogant boor! Crude lout! Braggart and boaster! To boast of what?" He snatched up a drinking horn. "See this?" he cried. "The name of Gast carved upon it and the letters worked in gold! See this cup! This bowl! These ornament my common table. My storehouse holds even finer, as you shall see. Goryon! Horseflesh is all he knows, and little enough of that!"

Fflewddur, meanwhile, had raised the harp to his shoulder and began to strike up a tune. "It's a small thing I composed myself," he explained. "Though I must say it's been cheered and praised by thousands . . ."

No sooner were the words past his lips than the harp bent like an overdrawn bow and a string broke with a loud twang. "Drat the thing!" muttered the bard. "Will it give me no peace? I swear it's getting worse. The slightest bit of color added to the facts and it costs me a string. Yes, as I meant to say, I know full half-a-dozen who deemed the song—ah— rather well done." With deftness born of long, sad practice, Fflewddur knotted up the broken string.

Taran, glancing around the Hall this while, was surprised to realize the plates and drinking horns of the guests were more than half-empty and, in fact, showed no sign of ever having been full. His perplex- 55 ity grew when the Steward returned to set the food-laden tray before Lord Gast, who planted his elbows on either side of it.

"Eat your fill," cried Gast to Taran and Gurgi, pushing a small hunch of gravy-spotted bread toward them and keeping the rest for himself. "Gast the Generous is ever openhanded! A sad fault that may turn me into a pauper, but it's my nature to be free with all my goods; I can't fight against it!"

"Generous?" Taran murmured under his breath to Fflewddur, while Gurgi, swallowing the skimpy fare, looked hopelessly around for more. "I think he'd make a miser seem a prodigal in comparison."

So passed the meal, with Gast loudly urging the companions to stuff themselves, yet all the while grudgingly offering them no more than a few morsels of stringy meat from the heaped platter. Only at the end, when Gast has swallowed all he could and his head nodded sleepily and his beard straggled into his drinking horn, were the companions able to down the meager leavings. At last, disheartened and with bellies still hollow, the three groped their way to a meanly furnished chamber, where they nevertheless dropped into sleep like stones.

In the morning Taran was impatient to start once more for Caer Cadarn, and Fflewddur agreed to ride with him. But Lord Gast would hear none of it until the companions marveled at his storerooms. The cantrev lord flung open chests of goblets, ornaments, weapons, horse trappings, and many things Taran judged of high value, but in such a muddled heap that he could scarcely tell one from another. Among all these goods Taran's eyes lingered on a gracefully fashioned wine bowl, the most beautiful Taran had ever seen. He had, however, little chance to admire it, for the cantrev lord quickly thrust a garishly ornamented horse bridle into Taran's hands and as quickly replaced it with a pair of stirrups which he praised equally.

"That wine bowl is worth all the rest put together," Fflewddur whispered to Taran, as Lord Gast now led the three companions from the storehouse to a large cow pen just outside the barricade. "I recognize the work from the hand of Annlaw Clay-Shaper, a master craftsman, the most skilled potter in Prydain. I swear his wheel is enchanted! Poor Gast!" Fflewddur added. "To count himself rich and know so little of what he owns!"

"But how has he gained such treasure?" Taran said.

"On that score, I should hesitate to ask," Fflewddur murmured with a grin. "Very likely the same way Goryon gained your horse."

"And this," cried the cantrev lord, halting beside a black cow who stood peacefully grazing amid the rest of the herd, "and this is Cornillo, the finest cow in all the land!"

Taran could not gainsay the words of the cantrev lord, for Cornillo shone as if she had been polished and her short, curving horns sparkled in the sun.

Lord Gast proudly stroked the animal's sleek flanks. "Gentle as a lamb! Strong as an ox! Swift as a horse and wise as an owl!" Gast went on, while Cornillo, calmly munching her cud, turned patient eyes to Taran, as though hoping not to be mistaken for anything other than a cow.

"She leads my cattle," declared Lord Gast, "better than any herdsman can. She'll pull a plow or turn a grist mill, if need be. Her calves are always twins! As for milk, she gives the sweetest! Cream, every drop! So rich the dairy maids can scarcely churn it!"

Cornillo blew out her breath almost in a sigh, switched her tail, and went back to grazing. From the pasture Lord Gast pressed the companions to the hen roost, and from there to the hawk mews, and the morning was half-spent and Taran had begun to despair of ever leaving the stronghold, when Gast finally ordered their mounts readied.

Fflewddur, Taran saw, still rode Llyan, the huge, golden-tawny cat who had saved the companions' lives on the Isle of Mona. "Yes, I decided to keep her—rather, she's decided to keep me," said the bard, as Llyan, recognizing Taran, padded forward and began happily rubbing her head against his shoulder. "She loves the harp more than ever," Fflewddur went on. "Can't hear enough of it." No sooner did he say this than Llyan flicked her long whiskers and turned to give the bard a forceful nudge; so that Fflewddur then and there had to unsling his instrument and strike a few chords, while Llyan, purring loudly, blinked fondly at him with great yellow eyes.

"Farewell," called the cantrev lord as the companions mounted. "At the stronghold of Gast the Generous you'll ever find an openhanded welcome!"

"It's a generosity that could starve us to death," Taran, laughing, remarked to the bard as they rode eastward again. "Gast thinks himself openhanded, as Goryon thinks himself valorous; and as far as I can judge, neither one has the truth of it. Yet," he added, "they both seem pleased with themselves. Indeed, is a man truly what he sees himself to be?"

"Only if what he sees is true," answered Fflewddur. "If there's too great a difference between his own opinion and the facts—ah—then, my friend, I should say that such a man had no more substance to him than Goryon's giants!

"But don't judge them too harshly," the bard 59

went on. "These cantrev nobles are much alike, prickly as porcupines one moment and friendly as puppies the next. They all hoard their possessions, yet they can be generous to a fault if the mood strikes them. As for valor, they're no cowards. Death rides in the saddle with them and they count it nothing, and in battle I've seen them gladly lay down their lives for a comrade. At the same time," he added, "it's also been my experience, in all my wanderings, that the further from the deed, the greater it grows, and the most glorious battle is the one longest past. So it's hardly surprising how many heroes you run into.

"Had they harps like mine," said Fflewddur, warily glancing at his instrument, "what a din you'd hear from every stronghold in Prydain!"

CHAPTER IV

A matter of Cows

Late that afternoon the companions sighted the crimson banner of the House of Smoit, its black bear emblem flying bravely above the towers of Caer Cadarn. Unlike the palisaded strongholds of the cantrev lords, Smoit's castle was a fortress with walls of hewn stone and iron-studded gates thick enough to withstand all attack; the chips in the stones and the dents in the portal told Taran the castle had indeed thrown back not a few assaults. For the three travelers, however, the gates were flung open willingly and an honor guard of spearmen hastened to escort the companions.

The red-bearded King sat at the dining table in his Great Hall, and from the array of dishes, platters, and drinking horns both full and empty Taran judged Smoit could scarcely have left off eating since morning. Seeing the companions, the King leaped from his throne of oakwood, fashioned in the shape of a gigantic bear looking much like Smoit himself.

"My body and bones!" Smoit roared so loudly the dishes rattled on the table. "It's better than a 61 feast to see all of you!" His battle-scarred face beamed with delight and he flung his burly arms around the companions in a joint-cracking hug. "Scrape out a tune from that old pot of yours," he cried to Fflewddur. "A merry tune for a merry meeting! And you, my lad," he went on, seizing Taran's shoulders with his heavy, red-furred hands, "when last we met you looked scrawny as a plucked chicken. And your shaggy friend—what, has he rolled in the bushes all the way from Caer Dallben?"

Smoit clapped his hands, shouted for more food and drink, and would hear nothing of Taran's news until the companions had eaten and the King had downed another full meal.

"The Mirror of Llunet?" said Smoit, when Taran at last was able to tell of his quest. "I've heard of no such thing. As well seek a needle in a haystack as a looking glass in the Llawgadarn Mountains." The King's heavy brow furrowed and he shook his head. "The Llawgadarns rise in the land of the Free Commots, and whether the folk there will be of a mind to help you . . ."

"The Free Commots?" Taran asked. "I've heard them named, but know little else about them."

"They're hamlets and small villages," Fflewddur put in. "They start to the east of the Hill Cantrevs and spread as far as Great Avren. I've never journeyed there myself; the Free Commots are a bit far even for my ramblings. But the land itself is the pleasantest in Prydain—fair hills and dales, rich soil to farm, and sweet grass for grazing. There's iron for good blades, gold and silver for fine ornaments. Annlaw Clay-Shaper is said to dwell among the Commot folk, as do many other craftsmen: master weavers, metalsmiths—from time out of mind their skills have been the Commots' pride."

"A proud folk they are," said Smoit. "And a stiff-necked breed. They bow to no cantrev lords, but only to the High King Math himself."

"No cantrev lords?" asked Taran, puzzled. "Who, then, rules them?"

"Why, they rule themselves," answered Smoit. "Strong and steadfast they are, too. And, by my beard, I'm sure there's more peace and neighborliness in the Free Commots than anywhere else in Prydain. And so what need have they for kings or lords? When you come to the meat of it," he added, "a king's strength lies in the will of those he rules."

Taran, who had been listening closely to these words of Smoit, nodded his head. "I had not thought of it thus," he said, half to himself. "Indeed, true allegiance is only given willingly."

"Enough talk!" cried Smoit. "It hurts my head and dries my gullet. Let's have more meat and drink. Forget the Mirror. Tarry with me in my cantrev, lad. We'll ride to the hunt, feast, and make merry. You'll put more flesh on your bones here than scrambling about on a fool's errand. And that, my boy, is good counsel to you."

Nevertheless, when he finally saw that Taran would not be dissuaded, Smoit goodnaturedly agreed to give the companions all they needed for the journey. Next morning, after a huge breakfast, which Smoit declared would serve to whet their appetites for dinner, the King threw open his storehouse to them and went with them to be sure they chose the best of gear.

Taran had only begun sorting through coils of rope, saddlebags, and harness leather when one of the castle guards burst into the storeroom, calling, "Sire! A horseman of Lord Gast is come. Raiders from Lord Goryon's stronghold have stolen Gast's prize cow and the rest of the herd with her!"

"My pulse!" roared Smoit. "My breath and blood!" The King's tangled bush of eyebrows knotted and his face turned as red as his beard. "How does he dare stir trouble in my cantrev!"

"The men of Gast have armed. They ride against Goryon," the guard hastened on. "Gast craves your help. Will you speak to his messenger?"

"Speak to him?" bellowed Smoit. "I'll clap his master in irons for breaking the peace. And worse! For breaking it without my leave!"

64

"Put Gast in irons?" Taran asked with some perplexity. "But Goryon stole his cow . . ."

"*His* cow?" cried Smoit. "His cow, indeed! Gast stole her from Goryon himself last year. And before that, the other way around. Neither of them knows whose beast it rightly is. Those two brawlers have ever been at loggerheads. Now the warm weather heats their blood again. But I'll cool their tempers. In my dungeon! Gast and Goryon both!"

Smoit snatched up a mighty double-edged battle axe. "I'll fetch them back by the ears!" he roared. "They know my dungeons; they've been there often enough. Who rides with me?"

"I will!" cried Fflewddur, his eyes lighting up. "Great Belin, a Fflam never shuns a fight!"

"If you ask our help, Sire," Taran began, "we give it willingly. But . . ."

"Mount up, then, my lad!" shouted Smoit. "You'll see justice done. And I'll have peace between Gast and Goryon if I have to break their heads to gain it!"

Swinging his battle axe, Smoit bolted from the store-room bellowing orders right and left. A dozen warriors sprang to horse. Smoit leaped astride a tall, barrel-chested steed, whistled through his teeth almost loudly enough to break them, and waved his men onward; amid the shouting and confusion

Taran, bewildered, found himself atop Melynlas galloping across the courtyard and out the castle gate.

The red-bearded King set such a pace through the valleys that it put even Llyan on her mettle to keep up; while Gurgi, with most of the wind pounded out of him, clung to the neck of his frantically galloping pony. Smoit's war horse was in a lather, and so was Melynlas before the cantrev King signaled a halt.

"To meat!" Smoit cried, swinging out of the saddle and looking as unwearied as if he had just begun a morning's trot. The companions, still catching their breath, had by no means found their appetites, but Smoit clapped his hands to the heavy bronze belt around his middle. "Hunger makes a man gloomy and saps all the spirit from a battle."

"Sire, must we battle with Lord Gast?" Taran asked with some concern, for Smoit's war band numbered only the dozen who had ridden from Caer Cadarn. "And if Lord Goryon's men have armed, we may be too few to stand against all of them."

"Battle?" Smoit retorted. "No, more's the pity. I'll have those troublemakers by the nose and into my dungeons before nightfall. They'll do as I command. I'm their king, by my beard! There's brawn enough here," he added, shaking a mighty fist, "to make them remember it."

"And yet," Taran ventured to say. "You yourself told me a king's true strength lay in the will of those he ruled."

"How's that?" cried Smoit, who had settled his bulk against a tree trunk and was about to attack the joint of meat he had pulled from his saddlebag. "Don't puzzle me with my own words! My body and bones, a king is a king!"

"I meant only that you've locked Gast and Goryon in your dungeon many times before," Taran answered. "And still they quarrel. Is there no way to keep peace between them? Or make them understand . . ."

"I'll reason them reasons!" bellowed Smoit, clutching his battle axe. He knitted his jutting brows. "But, true enough it is," he admitted, frowning and seeming to chew at the thought as if it were gristle in his meat, "they go surly to the dungeon and surly leave it. You've struck on something, my lad. The dungeon's useless against that pair. And, my pulse, I know why! It needs more dampness, more draught. So be it! I'll have the place well watered down tonight."

Taran was about to remark that his own thought was otherwise, but Fflewddur called out and pointed to a horseman galloping across the meadow. 67

"He wears the colors of Goryon," shouted Smoit, jumping to his feet, still holding the joint in one hand and the battle axe in the other. Two of the warriors quickly mounted and, drawing swords, spurred to engage the rider. But the horseman, brandishing his weapon hilt downward, cried out that he bore tidings from the cantrev lord.

"You rogue!" Smoit bellowed, dropping both meat and axe and collaring the rider to haul him bodily from the saddle. "What other mischief's afoot? Speak! Give me your news, man, or I'll have it out of you along with your gizzard!"

"Sire!" gasped the messenger, "Lord Gast attacks in strength. My Lord Goryon is hard-pressed; he has ordered more of his warriors to arm and calls on you to help him as well."

"What of the cows?" cried Smoit. "Has Gast won them back? Does Goryon still hold them?"

"Neither, Sire," answered the messenger as well as he could with Smoit shaking him between every word. "Lord Gast attacked Lord Goryon to regain his own herd and take Lord Goryon's, too. But as they fought, all the beasts frighted and ran off. The cows? Sire, both herds are gone, lost, every soul of them, and Cornillo herself!"

"Let that be the end of it!" declared Smoit, 68 "and a good lesson for all cow-robbers. Gast and

Goryon shall cry peace and I'll spare them from my dungeon."

"Sire, the fighting grows hotter," the messenger said urgently. "Neither one will leave off. Each blames the other for loss of his herd. Lord Goryon swears vengeance on Lord Gast; and Lord Gast swears vengeance on Lord Goryon."

"They've both been itching for battle," Smoit burst out. "Now they find their excuse!" He summoned one of his warriors, ordering him to take Goryon's messenger to Caer Cadarn, there to be held as hostage. "To horse, the rest of you," Smoit commanded. "My body and bones, we'll see sport after all." He gripped his axe. "Oh, there'll be heads broken today!" he cried with relish, and his battered face brightened as if he were on his way to a feast.

"The bards will sing of this," exclaimed Fflewddur, carried away by Smoit's ardor. "A Fflam in the thick of battle! The thicker the better!" The harp shuddered and a string snapped in two. "I mean," Fflewddur hastily added, "I hope we're not too badly outnumbered."

"Sire," Taran called as Smoit strode to his war horse. "If Gast and Goryon won't stop because their herds are lost, shouldn't we try to find the cows?"

"Yes, yes!" Gurgi put in. "Find cows gone with strayings! And put an end to fightings and smitings!" 69

·But Smoit had already mounted and was shouting for the war band to follow; and Taran could do no more than gallop after him. To which stronghold Smoit was leading them, Taran did not know. As far as Smoit was concerned, Taran decided, it made little difference whether Gast or Goryon fell first into the King's hands.

In a while, however, Taran recognized the path he and Gurgi had taken from Aeddan's farm, and he judged now that Smoit would make for Goryon's stronghold. But as they pounded across an open field, the King veered sharply left and Taran glimpsed a troop of mounted warriors some distance away.

At the sight of their banners, Smoit bellowed furiously and spurred his steed to overtake the horsemen. But the riders, themselves galloping at top speed, quickly vanished into the woodland. Smoit reined up, shouting after them and shaking his huge fist.

"Has Goryon put more warriors in the fray?" roared Smoit, his face crimson. 'Then Gast has done the same! Those louts wore his colors!"

"Sire," Taran began, "if we can find the cows—"

"Cows!" burst out Smoit. "There's more than cows in this, my lad. Such a brawl can spread like a spark through tinder. Those thick-skulled ruffians will set the whole of Cadiffor ablaze and next thing you know we'll all be at one another's throats! But, by my beard, they'll learn my fist smites harder than theirs!"

Smoit hesitated and his face darkened with deep concern. He scowled and tugged at his beard. "The lords of the next cantrev," he muttered. "They'll not stand idle, but strike against us when they see we're fighting each other!"

"But the cows," Taran urged. "The three of us can seek them, while you—"

"The dungeon!" cried Smoit. "I'll have Gast and Goryon in it before their squabble gets further out of hand."

Smoit clapped heels to his horse and charged forward, making no attempt to hold to any pathway, dashing at breakneck speed through bramble and thicket. With the companions and the train of warriors pelting behind, Smoit clattered over the stones of a riverbank and plunged his horse into the swift current. The King had ill chosen his fording place, for in another moment Taran found himself in water up to his saddlehorn. Smoit, shouting impatiently, pressed on across the river. Taran saw the King rise up in his stirrups to beckon his followers and urge more haste. But an instant later the war horse lost footing and lurched sideways; steed and rider toppled with a mighty splash, and before Taran could 71 spur Melynlas to him, Smoit had been torn loose from his mount and, like a barrel with arms and legs, was being borne quickly downstream.

Behind Taran some of the warriors had turned back, seeking to overtake the King by following along the riverbank. Taran, closer to the opposite bank, urged all strength from Melynlas, leaped from the saddle to dry ground, and raced along the shore after Smoit. The sound of rushing water filled his ears, and with dismay Taran realized the King was being pulled relentlessly to a waterfall. Heart bursting in his chest, Taran doubled his pace; though before he could set foot in the rapids, he saw the King's red beard sink below the churning water, and he cried out in despair as Smoit vanished over the brink.

CHAPTER V

A Judgment

aran scrambled down the rocks jutting beside the high cascade. In a pool hammered into white spray he could hardly make out Smoit's burly form spinning in the eddies. Heedless of the pounding water, Taran pitched through the falls and sprang into the pool. He groped for Smoit's belt and seized it at last. Battling the whirlpool and nearly drowning himself with his own efforts, Taran painfully strove to drag the half-conscious King into the shallows.

Smoit was bleeding heavily from the forehead and his ruddy face had gone chalky pale. Taran tugged at the King's waterlogged bulk, hauling him safely from the rolling waters. In another moment Gurgi and Fflewddur were beside him, helping to drag the King ashore. Smoit, like a beached whale, collapsed on the bank.

Gurgi, moaning anxiously, loosened the King's garments, while Taran and the bard hastily saw to Smoit's injuries.

"He can count himself lucky he's only cracked his skull and half his ribs," Fflewddur said. "Another 73 man would have been snapped in two. But we're in a fine pickle," he added under his breath to Taran, glancing at the warriors who had come to gather near the unconscious Smoit. "He'll not lay Gast or Goryon by the heels now. He needs more healing than we can give. We'd best take him to Caer Cadarn."

Taran shook his head. He remembered Smoit's words about the neighboring cantrev lords who would seize the opportunity to attack. It was in his mind, too, that finding Cornillo could best bring Gast and Goryon to terms and thus end their battle. But his thoughts were as tangled as Orddu's weaving and he fervently wished himself in the place of Smoit, whose unconsciousness at that moment seemed a most enviable state.

"Aeddan's farmhold is closer," Taran said. "We'll bring him there and Gurgi shall stay with him. You and I must seek out Gast and Goryon and do what we can to stop their quarrel. As for Cornillo and the herd, I doubt we may hope to find them."

The companions, tearing their cloaks into strips, set about binding up Smoit's wounds. The King's eyelids fluttered and he groaned loudly.

"Give me to eat!" gasped Smoit. "I may be half-drowned, but I'll not be half-starved." He put a hand on Taran's shoulder. "Good lad, good lad.

You've saved my life. Another moment and I'd have been beaten into a pudding. Claim any favor, it is yours."

"I ask none," Taran replied, knotting the bandages around Smoit's huge chest. "Alas," he murmured, "what I most want, none can grant."

"No matter," panted Smoit. "What you wish of me, you shall have."

"Sire, you cannot travel far," Taran began as Smoit tried painfully to climb to his feet. "Give us leave to ride with your warriors and—"

"Kind master! Hear!" Gurgi called excitedly. "Hear with listenings!"

Llyan, too, had caught some sound, for her ears cupped forward and her whiskers twitched.

"It's my gizzard calling for meat and drink!" cried Smoit. "Loud it must be, for I'm empty as a drum!"

"No, no," shouted Gurgi, seizing Taran's arm and drawing him past the trees along the riverside. "Gurgi hears no thrummings and drummings but cooings and mooings!"

Leaning on the bard, Smoit stumbled after them. Gurgi had spoken the truth; the creature's sharp ears had not deceived him. Now Taran himself heard a faint lowing. Gurgi raced toward the sound. Beyond the trees the land dipped into a shady dell watered by a streamlet. Taran cried aloud. There stood the herd, grazing calmly around Cornillo.

"My pulse!" bellowed Smoit, so loudly that a dozen horned heads turned and stared as alarmed as if some strange new kind of bull had burst into their quiet pasture.

"Great Belin!" cried Fflewddur. "Cornillo's led them all to safety. She's wiser than either of her masters!"

Cornillo raised her head as Taran hurried to her side. She blew out her breath gently and rolled her eyes in a look of long-suffering patience. Smoit, heedless of his grievous bruises, clapped his hands triumphantly and shouted at the top of his voice for his warriors.

"Sire, let us drive the herd to Aeddan's farm," Taran urged. "Your own hurts must be tended better than we've done."

"Drive them where you please, lad," answered Smoit. "My body and bones, we have them now! That will fetch Gast and Goryon to me at a gallop!" He summoned two horsemen, commanding them to bear a message to the cantrev lords. "Tell those two troublemakers where I'll await them," cried Smoit. "And tell each to call truce, for his cows are found!"

"And Gurgi found them!" shouted Gurgi, capering wildly. "Yes, yes! Bold, clever, sharp-eared

Gurgi finds all that is lost, oh, yes!" He flung his hairy arms around himself and seemed close to bursting with pride and delight at his own deed. "Oh, bards will sing of clever Gurgi with rantings and chantings!"

"I'm sure they will, old friend," Taran said. "You've found the herd. But don't forget we still have Gast and Goryon to deal with—and there's only one Cornillo."

The cows were at first reluctant to quit the dell, but after much coaxing Taran was able to lead Cornillo along the valley pathways toward Aeddan's farm. The others followed her, lowing and tossing their horns; it was a strange procession that wended its way across the meadows and rolling hillocks. Smoit's warriors rode on either side of the herd, and the red-bearded King himself brandished a spear as if it were a drover's staff; Llyan padded after the cattle, alert for strays; and Gurgi perched proud as a shaggy rooster on Cornillo's back.

When Aeddan's hut came in sight Taran galloped ahead calling to the farmer, but he had no sooner dismounted when the door burst open and he fell back, surprised. Aeddan stood with a rusted sword in his hand. Behind the farmer, Taran glimpsed Alarca weeping into her apron.

"Is this how you repay kindness?" Aeddan 77

cried, recognizing Taran immediately. His eyes blazed as he pointed the ancient weapon at the approaching war band. "Do you come with them to spoil our land? Begone! It is already done!"

"How then?" Taran stammered, shocked at these words from one he held to be a friend. "I ride with King Smoit and his men. We seek peace between Gast and Goryon—"

"Does it matter whose warriors trampled my crops?" Aeddan flung back. "What Gast has destroyed, Goryon has doubly destroyed, warring back and forth across my field till not a blade of wheat stands! Battle is their pride, but my farm is my life. Do they seek vengeance? I sought only a harvest." In the weariness of despair Aeddan bowed his head and cast his sword to the ground.

Taran stared in dismay at the field where Aeddan had so painfully labored. The hooves of steeds had churned the earth to mud, uprooting the young shoots which now lay torn to shreds. The harvest on which Aeddan had staked his livelihood would never come, and Taran felt the farmer's heartbreak as if it were his own.

Before he could speak, a troop of horsemen galloped from the woods edging the farm. Taran recognized Lord Goryon at their head. In another
moment Lord Gast and his riders appeared. Catch-

ing sight of his rival, the cantrev lord spurred his mount and galloped frantically to the cottage, flung himself out of the saddle, and with a furious shout raced toward Goryon.

"Robber!" cried Gast. "Do you mean to steal Cornillo from me again?"

"Thief!" cried Goryon. "I took what was mine to begin with!"

"Liar!" roared Gast. "Never was she yours!"

"Insults! Insolence!" roared Goryon, his face turning purple, his hand snatching for his sword.

"Be silent!" bellowed Smoit. He shook his battle axe at the cantrev lords. "Your King speaks! How dare you quarrel and insult each other, you pigheaded brawlers!" Smoit gestured to his warriors, who strode to seize Gast and Goryon. The riders of the two war bands cried out angrily and made to unsheathe their swords; for an instant Taran feared another battle would rage then and there. But Smoit's warriors stood their ground, and the sight of the enraged King himself caused the horsemen to draw back submissively.

"My dungeon will teach you to be good neighbors," cried Smoit. "You'll stay there till you learn. As for Cornillo—I've split my skull, cracked my bones, and ridden to the edge of starvation this day, and so I claim her for myself! A prize of war! 79

And small recompense it is for the vexation you've given me! Another day and you'd have set the whole cantrev ablaze!"

At this, Gast and Goryon both roared in furious protest; and Taran could no longer hold his tongue. He strode to the King's side.

"Sire, even a lifetime in your dungeon will not raise one grain of wheat on a ruined field. Aeddan has lost all he hoped to gain, one harvest to keep himself and his wife alive. You offered me a favor," Taran went on. "I refused it then; will you let me claim it now?"

"Ask what you please my lad," replied Smoit. "It is already given."

Taran hesitated a moment as he stepped forward and stood facing the cantrev lords. Then he turned to Smoit. "I ask you this," he said. "Set Gast and Goryon free."

While Smoit blinked in astonishment, Goryon, glimpsing Taran for the first time, exclaimed, "It's the pig-keeper who cozened me out of my horse!. I took him for a lout, but he asks a noble favor. Grant it, Smoit. He speaks wisdom!"

"Set them free," Taran continued, "to labor beside Aeddan and strive to mend what they have destroyed."

"What?" cried Gast. "I took him for a hero, but he's no more than a lout! How dare he ask Gast the Generous to delve the ground like a mole and for no reward!"

"Impudence! Impertinence! Insolence!" shouted Goryon. "I'll not have a pig-keeper pass judgment on Goryon the Valorous!"

"Nor on Gast the Generous!" exclaimed Gast.

"Pass judgment on yourselves, then," Taran answered, picking up two handfuls of earth and torn shoots and holding them before the furious cantrev lords. "This is what remains of Aeddan's livelihood. As well take a sword and slay him. Look on this, Lord Goryon, for there is more truth here than in your tales of giants and monsters. And this he treasured, Lord Gast, more than you treasure any of your possessions—and it was more truly his own, for he toiled to make it so."

Gast and Goryon had fallen silent; the two rough cantrev lords stared at the ground like sheepish boys.

Aeddan and his wife looked on without speaking.

"The lad has a better head on his shoulders than I do," exclaimed Smoit, "and his judgment is wiser. Kinder, too, for my choice would have been the dungeon, not the delving!"

The cantrev lords reluctantly nodded agreement.

Taran turned to Smoit. "The rest of my favor

is this: Grant most where need is greatest. Do you claim Cornillo for your own? Sire, give her to Aeddan."

"Give up Cornillo?" Smoit began, sputtering and choking. "My prize of war. . ." He finally nodded his head. "So be it, lad."

"Aeddan shall keep her," Taran went on, "and Gast and Goryon shall have her next calves."

"What of my herd?" cried Goryon.

"And mine!" cried Gast. "They're so mixed together no man can tell his own from another's."

"Lord Goryon shall divide the herds in equal portions," Taran said.

"He shall not!" Lord Gast broke in. "He'll give me all the scrawny ones and keep the fat for himself. It's I who'll divide them!"

"Not so!" shouted Goryon. "You'll fob off none of your rawboned creatures on me!"

"Lord Goryon shall divide the herds," Taran repeated. "But Lord Gast shall be first to choose his half."

"Well said!" Smoit burst out, roaring with laughter. "My breath and blood, you have them there! Goryon divides and Gast chooses! Ho, oho! It takes two thieves to strike an honest bargain!"

Aeddan and Alarca had come to stand before

Taran and King Smoit. "Who you may truly be, I do

not know," the farmer said to Taran. "But you be-friended me far better than I befriended you."

"Oh, wisdom of kindly master!" cried Gurgi, as the cantrev lords set about dividing their herds and Smoit's warriors made ready to return to Caer Cadarn. "Gurgi finds cows, but only wise master knows what to do with them!"

"If indeed I did rightly," Taran replied, "Gast and Goryon will be waiting for Cornillo's calves. Gast said they were always twins. I only hope," he added with a grin, "that she doesn't disappoint us."

It was long after nightfall when the compan-ions at last reached Caer Cadarn. Fflewddur and Gurgi were too exhausted to do more than fling themselves onto their couches. Taran would gladly have followed them, but Smoit took his arm and drew him to the Great Hall.

"Count your day well spent, my lad," cried Smoit. "You've spared the cantrev from a war and me from being drubbed into jelly. As for Gast and Goryon, how long they'll stay at peace with each other I'll not guess. But you've taught me one thing: My dungeons are useless. My body and bones, I'll have them walled up directly. From this day I'll try my hand at speaking instead of smiting!

"And yet, lad," Smoit went on, furrowing his brow, "my wits are slow. I need no man to tell me that, and I am easier in my mind when I have a blade in my hand. Will you return favor for favor? Stay with me in Cantrev Cadiffor."

"Sire," Taran answered, "I seek to learn who my kinsmen are. I cannot . . ."

"Kinsmen!" shouted Smoit, slapping his great girth. "There's enough of me to make all the kinsmen you could want! Hear me well," he added, his voice quieter now, "a widower am I, and childless. Do you yearn for parents? No less do I yearn for a son. When the horn of Gwyn the Hunter sounds for me, there shall be none to take my place, and none would I choose but you. Stay, lad, and you shall one day be King of Cadiffor."

"King of Cadiffor?" Taran cried. His heart leaped. What need to seek the Mirror when he could offer Eilonwy a royal throne, the proudest gift he could ever lay at her feet? Taran King of Cadiffor. The words rang more sweetly in his ears than Taran Assistant Pig-Keeper. Yet suddenly his joy turned cold. While Eilonwy might honor his rank, could she respect him for abandoning his quest even before it had begun? Could he respect himself? For a long while Taran did not answer, then with fond admira-

tion he turned his eyes to Smoit.

"The honor you would give me," Taran began, "there is nothing I would value more highly. Yes—I long to accept it." His voice faltered. "Yet I would rather hold kingship by right of noble birth, not as a gift. It may be," he went on slowly, "that in truth I am nobly born. If it should prove thus, then gladly would I rule Cadiffor."

"How then!" cried Smoit. "My body and bones, I'd rather see a wise pig-keeper on my throne than a blood prince who's a fool!"

"But there is this, as well," Taran answered. "It is in my heart to learn the truth about myself. I will not stop short of it. Were I to do so, who I truly am would forever be unknown and through all my life I would feel a part of me lacking."

At these words Smoit's battle-scarred face fell with sadness and regretfully he bowed his head. But after a moment he clapped Taran heartily on the back. "My breath, blood, and beard!" he cried. "You've a will to chase the wild goose, will-o'-the-wisp, looking-glass, or whatever it may be; and I'll say no more to keep you from it. Seek it out, lad! Whether or not you find it, come back and Cadiffor will welcome you. But hasten, for if Gast and Goryon are ever at loggerheads again, I'll not vouch for how much of the cantrev will be left!"

Thus Taran, with Gurgi and Fflewddur 85

Fflam, set off once more. In his secret heart Taran cherished the hope he might return to Smoit's realm with proud tidings of his parentage. Yet he did not foresee how long it would be until he set foot in Cantrev Cadiffor again.

CHAPTER VI

A Frog

From Caer Cadarn the companions made good progress and within a few days crossed the Ystrad River, where Fflewddur led them for a time along the farther bank before turning northeastward through the Hill Cantrevs. Unlike the Valley Cantrevs, these lands were grayish and flinty. What might once have been fair pastureland Taran saw to be overlaid with brush, and the long reaches of forest were close-grown and darkly tangled.

Fflewddur admitted his roving seldom brought him to these parts. "The cantrev nobles are as glum as their domains. Play your merriest tune and the best you can hope for is a sour smile. Yet, if the old lore is true, these realms were as rich as any in Prydain. The sheep of the Hill Cantrevs—Great Belin, it's said they had fleece so thick you could sink your arm in it up to the elbow! Nowadays, alas, they tend to be a little scruffy."

"Aeddan told me Arawn Death-Lord stole many secrets from the farmers of the valley," Taran 87 replied. "Surely he robbed the shepherds of the Hill Cantrevs as well."

Fflewddur nodded. "Few treasures he hasn't spoiled or stolen save those of the Fair Folk, and even Arawn might think twice before trifling with them. Be that as it may," he went on, "I'd not change the Northern Realms, where my own kingdom is, for any of these. There, my boy, we raise no sheep, but famous bards and warriors! Naturally, the House of Fflam has held its throne there for—well, for a remarkably long time. In the veins of a Fflam," declared the bard, "flows royal blood of the Sons of Don! Prince Gwydion himself is my kinsman. Distant —distant, it's true," he added hastily, "but a kinsman nonetheless."

"Gurgi does not care for famous sheep or fleecy bards," Gurgi wistfully murmured. "He is happy at Caer Dallben, oh, yes, and wishes he is soon there."

"As for that," answered Fflewddur, "I'm afraid you'll have hard travel before you see home again. It's anyone's guess how long it will take to find your mysterious Mirror. I'll go with you as far as I can," he said to Taran, "though sooner or later I shall have to get back to my kingdom. My subjects are always impatient for my return . . ."

The harp shuddered violently as a string snapped in two. Fflewddur's face reddened. "Ahem," he said, "yes, what I meant was: I'll be anxious to see *them* again. The truth of it is, I often have the feeling they manage quite well even when I'm not there. Still, a Fflam is dutiful!"

The companions halted while Fflewddur slid from Llyan's back and squatted on the turf to repair his broken string. From his jacket the bard took the large key which he used to tighten the harp's wooden pegs, and began patiently retuning the instrument.

A raucous cry made Taran glance quickly skyward. "It's Kaw!" he exclaimed, pointing to the winged shape plummeting swiftly toward the companions. Gurgi shouted joyfully and clapped his hands as the crow alighted on Taran's wrist.

"So you've found us, old friend," cried Taran, delighted to have the crow with him once again. "Tell me," he went on quickly, "how does Eilonwy fare? Does she miss—all of us?"

"Princess!" Kaw croaked, beating his wings. "Princess! Eilonwy! Taran!" He clacked his beak, hopped up and down on Taran's wrist, and set up such a jabbering and chattering that Taran could barely make out one word from another. The best he could understand was that Eilonwy's indignation at being forced to learn royal behavior had by no means dwindled, and that indeed she missed him—tidings that both cheered Taran and sharpened his yearning for the golden-haired Princess.

In the cavern on Mona, Kaw also managed to convey, Glew the giant had been restored to his original size by Dallben's potion.

Kaw himself was in the best of spirits. Still gabbling at the top of his voice, he flapped his glossy black wings, hopped from Taran's wrist to greet the other companions, and even perched on Llyan's head, where he busily ran his beak through the great cat's tawny fur.

"His eyes will help our search," Taran said to Fflewddur, who had left his harp to come and stroke the bird's sleek feathers. "Kaw can scout the land better than any of us."

"So he can," agreed Fflewddur, "if he has a mind to and if you can make him heed you. Otherwise the scamp will have his beak in everyone's business but his own."

"Yes, yes," Gurgi added, shaking a finger at the crow. "Heed commands of kindly master! Help him with flyings and spyings, not pryings and lyings!"

In answer, the crow impudently thrust out a sharp black tongue. With a flirt of his tail he fluttered to the harp and began rapidly twanging the strings with his beak. At the bard's cry of protest, Kaw hopped from the instrument's curved frame and snatched up the tuning key, which he began dragging across the turf.

"He's brazen as a magpie!" cried Fflewddur, setting off after the crow. "He's thieving as a jackdaw!"

No sooner did Fflewddur come within half a pace of him than Kaw nimbly hopped away again, bearing the key in his beak. Squawking merrily, the crow stayed always out of Fflewddur's grasp, and Taran could not help laughing at the sight of the long-shanked bard vainly racing in circles, while Kaw danced ahead of him. When Gurgi and Taran joined the pursuit and Taran's fingers had come within a hair's breadth of the crow's tail feathers, Kaw shot upwards and flapped teasingly a short distance into the woods. There he lighted on the gnarled branch of a tall, ancient oak, and peered with bright beady eyes at the companions gathered below.

"Come down," Taran ordered as sternly as he could, for the bird's comical antics made it impossible for him to be seriously angry. "I've tried to teach him to behave," Taran sighed, "but it's no use. He'll bring it back when he feels like it and not before."

"Hi, hi! Drop it!" called Fflewddur, waving his arms. "Drop it, I say!"

At this Kaw bobbed his head, hunched up his wings, and dropped the key—not into the bard's outstretched hands but into a hollow of the tree trunk.

"Dropped it! Dropped it!" croaked Kaw, rocking back and forth on the branch, jabbering and chuckling gleefully at his own jest.

Fflewddur snorted. "That bird's ill-mannered as a starling! He's had his merriment, now I shall have the toil." Muttering hard comments about the impudence of waggish crows, the bard flung his arms about the trunk and tried to haul himself upward. Less than halfway, his grip loosened and he came tumbling down to land heavily amid the roots.

"A Fflam is agile!" Fflewddur panted, ruefully rubbing his back. "Great Belin, there's not a tree I can't climb—ah, except this one." He mopped his brow and glared at the high trunk.

"Gurgi climbs, yes, yes!" cried Gurgi, springing to the oak. With shaggy arms and legs working all at once, in a trice the creature clambered up the tree. While Fflewddur shouted encouragement, Gurgi thrust a skinny hand into the hollow.

"Here is tuneful key, oh, yes!" he called. "Clever Gurgi finds it!" He stopped short. Taran saw the creature's face wrinkle in surprise and perplexity. Tossing the key down to Fflewddur, Gurgi turned once more to the hollow. "But what is this? What else does Gurgi find with gropings? Kindly master," he shouted, "here is strange something all set away in hidings!"

Taran saw the excited creature tuck an object under his arm and slide down the oak tree.

"See with lookings!" cried Gurgi as Taran and the bard pressed around him.

Kaw's prank was forgotten in the moment and the crow, not abashed whatever, flew to Taran's shoulder, stretched out his neck, and crowded forward as if determined to be first to glimpse Gurgi's discovery.

"Is it treasure?" Gurgi exclaimed. "Oh, treasure of great worth! And Gurgi finds it!" He stamped his feet wildly. "Open it, kindly master! Open and see what riches it holds!"

What Gurgi pressed into Taran's hand was a small, squat iron coffer no wider than Taran's palm. Its curved lid was heavily hinged, bound with iron strips, and secured by a stout padlock.

"Is it jewels with winkings and blinkings? Or gold with shimmerings and glimmerings?" cried Gurgi, as Taran turned the coffer over and over; Fflewddur, too, peered at it curiously.

"Well, friends," the bard remarked, "at least we'll have some reward for the trouble that pilfering jackdaw has given us. Though from the size of it, I fear it shan't be very much."

Taran, meantime, had been struggling with the lock which refused to give way. The lid resisted all his battering, and finally he had to set the coffer on the ground where Gurgi held it tightly while the bard and Taran pried at the hinges with the points of their swords. But the coffer was surprisingly strong, and it took all their strength and effort before the lid at last yielded and fell away with a loud, rasping snap. Within lay a packet of soft leather which Taran carefully untied.

"What is it? What is it?" yelped Gurgi, jumping up and down on one leg. "Let Gurgi see shining treasure!"

Taran laughed and shook his head. The packet held neither gold nor gems, but no more than a slender piece of bone as long as Taran's little finger. Gurgi groaned in disappointment.

Fflewddur snorted. "I should say our shaggy friend has found a very small hairpin or a very large toothpick. I doubt we'll have much use for either one."

Taran had not ceased examining the strange object. The sliver of bone was dry and brittle, bleached white and highly polished. Whether animal or human he could not tell. "What value can this have?" he murmured, frowning.

"Great value," replied Fflewddur, "if one should ever need a toothpick. Beyond that," he shrugged. "Keep it, if you like or toss it away; I can't see it would make any difference. Even the chest is beyond repair."

"But if it's worthless," Taran said, still studying the bone closely, "why should it be so carefully
94 locked up? And so carefully hidden?"

"It's been my long experience that people can be very odd about their belongings," said Fflewddur. "A favorite toothpick, a family heirloom—but, yes, I see what you're driving at. A Fflam is quick-thinking! Whoever put it away didn't want it found. As I was about to remark, there's considerably more here than meets the eye."

"And yet," Taran began, "a hollow tree seems hardly the safest place to keep anything."

"On the contrary," answered the bard. "What better way to hide something? Indoors, it could be found without too much difficulty. Bury it in the ground and there's the problem of moles, badgers, and all such. But a tree like this," he continued, glancing upward, "I doubt that anyone but Gurgi could climb it without a ladder, and it's hardly probable that anyone strolling through this forest would be carrying a ladder with them. If the birds or squirrels nest on top, they'd only cover it up all the more. No, whoever put it there gave the matter careful thought and took as much pains as if . . ."

Fflewddur's face paled. "As if . . ." He swallowed hard, choking on his own words. "Get rid of it" he whispered urgently. "Forget we ever found the thing. I can sniff enchantment a mile away. Toothpick, hairpin, or what have you, there's something queer about it." He shuddered. "As I've said time and time again: Don't meddle. You know my 95 mind on that score. Two things never mix: one is enchantments and the other is meddling with them."

Taran did not answer immediately, but stared for a time at the polished fragment. At last he said, "Whatever it may be, it's not ours to take. Yet, if there is enchantment, good or evil, dare we leave it?"

"Away with it!" cried Fflewddur. "If it's good there's no harm done. If it's evil there's no telling what beastly thing might happen. Put it back, by all means."

Taran reluctantly nodded. Wrapping the bone once more, he replaced it in the coffer, set the broken lid loosely on top, and asked Gurgi to return it to the hollow. Gurgi, who had been listening closely to Fflewddur's talk of enchantment, was loath even to touch the coffer; and only after much urging and pleading by the companions did he agree to do so. He hastily climbed the oak and scuttled down even faster than he had clambered up.

"And good riddance to it," muttered Fflewddur, striding as quickly as he could from the forest, Taran and Gurgi after him, the latter casting fearful backward glances until the oak was well out of sight.

The companions returned to their steeds and
prepared to mount. Fflewddur picked up his harp,

looked about him, and called, "I say, where's Llyan? Don't tell me she's wandered off."

Taran's alarm quickly changed to reassurance, for a moment later he saw the huge cat plunge from the underbrush and lope to Fflewddur, who clapped his hands and made loud whispering noises through his teeth.

"Sa! Sa! So there you are, old girl," cried the bard, beaming happily as Llyan frisked about him. "Now, what have *you* been after?"

"I think she's caught a—why, yes—she's caught a frog!" Taran exclaimed, catching sight of a pair of long legs with webbed feet dangling from Llyan's mouth.

"Yes, yes," put in Gurgi. "A froggie! A froggie with thumpings and jumpings!"

"I should hardly think so," said the bard. "We've seen no swamps or pools, and very little water at all, for the matter of that."

Proudly purring, Llyan dropped her burden at Fflewddur's feet. It was indeed a frog, and the biggest Taran had ever seen. The bard, after patting Llyan's head and fondly rubbing her ears, knelt and with a certain squeamishness picked up the motionless creature.

"Yes, well, I'm delighted, old girl," he said, holding it at arm's length between his thumb and forefinger. "It's lovely; I don't know how to thank 97 you. She often does this," he explained to Taran. "I don't mean dead frogs necessarily, but odds and ends —an occasional mouse, that sort of thing. Little gifts she fancies I might enjoy. A sign of affection. I always make a fuss over them. It's the thought, after all, that counts."

Taran, curious, took the frog from the bard's hand. Llyan, he saw, had carried the creature gently and had in no way harmed it. Instead, the frog had suffered from lack of water. Its skin, splotched in green and yellow, was sadly parched. Its legs feebly splayed; its webbed toes had begun to curl and wither like dry leaves; and its great bulging eyes were tightly shut. Regretfully, Taran was about to return the creature to the bushes when the faint tremor of a heartbeat touched his palm.

"Fflewddur, the poor thing's alive," Taran said. "There may still be time to save him."

The bard shook his head. "I doubt it. He's too much the worse for wear. A shame, for he's a jolly-looking fellow."

"Give poor froggie a drink," Gurgi suggested. "Give him water with sloshings and washings."

In Taran's hand the frog stirred as in a last, painful effort. One eye flickered, the wide mouth gaped, and its throat trembled like a faint pulse. **98** "Arrad!" croaked the frog.

"I say, there is life in him yet!" exclaimed Fflewddur. "But he must be desperately sick. I've never heard a frog make a noise like that."

"Urgghi!" the frog croaked. "Ood!"

The creature was struggling to make a further sound, but its croaking dwindled to a hoarse and scarcely audible rasping.

"Elpp! Elpp!"

"He is an odd one," remarked Fflewddur, as Taran, more puzzled than ever, held the frog close to his ear. The creature had forced its eyes open and stared at Taran with what seemed a most pitiful, pleading expression.

"I've known them to go 'chug-a-chug,'" continued Fflewddur, "and at times 'thonk.' But this fellow—if frogs could talk, I'd swear he was saying 'help'!"

Taran gestured the bard to silence. From deep in the frog's throat came another sound, hardly more than a whisper but clear and unmistakable. Taran's jaw fell. His eyes wide with bewilderment, he turned to Fflewddur. Barely able to speak, he held the frog in his outstretched hand and gasped, "It's Doli!"

CHAPTER VII

Friends in Danger

oli!" echoed the astonished bard, falling back a pace.
His eyes bulged like the frog's and he clapped his
hands to his head. "It can't be! Not Doli of the Fair
Folk! Not good old Doli!"

Gurgi had just then come up with a leather
water flask and, hearing Fflewddur's words, began
yelping in terror and dismay. Taran took the flask
from Gurgi's trembling hand, unstoppered it, and
with all haste began drenching the frog.

"Oh, terrible! Oh, horrible!" moaned Gurgi.
"Unlucky Doli! Unhappy dwarfish companion! But
how did this froggie swallow him with gulpings?"

Under the stream of water the frog had begun
to revive, and now kicked mightily with its long hind
legs.

"Skin! Skin!" came Doli's voice. "Pour it on my
skin! Not down my throat, you clot! Are you trying
to drown me?"

"Great Belin," murmured Fflewddur. "At first

I thought it was just a frog who happened to have the same name as Doli. But I'd know that temper anywhere."

"Doli!" Taran cried. "Is it really you?"

"Of course it is, you long-legged beanpole!" snapped Doli's voice. "Just because I look like a frog on the outside doesn't mean I'm not myself on the inside!"

Taran's head spun at the thought of Doli in this form. Gurgi was speechless, his eyes as round and wide open as his mouth. Fflewddur, as stunned as the other companions, had recovered somewhat from his first shock and now dropped to his hands and knees on the damp turf where Taran had set the frog.

"You've chosen a strange way to travel about," said Fflewddur. "Did you weary of turning yourself invisible? I can understand how that might be tiresome. But—a frog? Though you do make a handsome one. I remarked on it the moment I saw you."

The frog rolled up his eyes in utter exasperation and his green-spotted body began to swell as if it might burst. "Chosen? Do you think I chose this? I'm bewitched, you ninny! Can't you see that?"

Taran's heart skipped a beat. "Who bewitched you?" he cried, aghast at the weird fate which had befallen his old companion. "Was it Orddu? She's   101 threatened us before. Did you, too, journey to the Marshes?"

"Idiot! Numbskull!" retorted Doli. "I've better sense than to trifle with her."

"Who then has done this to you?" Taran exclaimed. "How can we help? Dallben surely has power against such enchantment. Have courage! We'll take you to him."

"No time!" Doli answered. "I don't know if Dallben can break the spell. I don't even know if King Eiddileg of the Fair Folk can do it. Right now it doesn't matter.

"If you want to help me," Doli went on, "dig a hole and put some water in it. I'm dry as a bone, and that's the worst thing that can happen to me—I mean, to a frog. I learned that quickly enough." He blinked at Fflewddur. "If that giant cat of yours hadn't found me, I'd be dead as a stump. Where did you ever get such a big one?"

"It's a long story," began the bard.

"Don't tell me then," snapped Doli. "As for what brings you here, of all places, you can explain when there's more time." He settled into the muddy basin Taran and Fflewddur had scraped out with their swords and filled with water from the flask. "Ah —ah, that's better. I owe you my life. Ah—what a relief. Thank you, friends, thank you."

"Doli, we can't let you stay in this plight," Taran insisted. "Tell us who cast this evil spell. We'll find him and make him lift it."

"At sword point, if need be!" cried Fflewddur. He stopped and peered with renewed fascination at Doli. "I say, old boy, what's it really like, being a frog? I've often wondered."

"Damp is what it's like," retorted Doli. "Damp! Clammy! If I thought turning myself invisible was uncomfortable, this is a hundred times worse. It's like—oh, don't boggle me with stupid questions! It doesn't matter. I'll manage somehow. There's more important work afoot.

"Yes, you can help me," Doli quickly went on. "If anyone can help at all. Strange things have been happening . . ."

"So it would seem," agreed the bard, "to say the very least."

"Fflewddur, let him speak," Taran broke in. "His life may be at stake."

"Strange things," Doli resumed. "Peculiar, unsettling. First, not long ago, word reached King Eiddileg in our realm at the bottom of Black Lake that someone had plundered a Fair Folk treasure trove. Broke into it! Made off with the most valuable gems. It's rarely happened in all the history of Prydain."

103

Fflewddur gave a whistle of surprise. "Knowing Eiddileg, I can imagine he was rather sour about it."

"Not for loss of the gems," replied Doli. "We've more than enough. It's that someone was able to find the trove in the first place; and, in the second, dared to lay hands on Fair Folk treasure. Most of you mortals have better sense."

"Could it have been Arawn or any of his servants?" Taran asked.

"I shouldn't think so," put in Fflewddur. "As I remarked only today, even the Lord of Annuvin would be more than cautious with Fair Folk."

"For once you're right," Doli answered. "No, not Arawn. We were sure of that. But we had only one report, incomplete, from a Fair Folk watcher in the Hill Cantrevs. No tidings from the guardian of the way post here—that, in itself, was very odd.

"Eiddileg sent a messenger to scout around and get to the root of things. He never came back. Not a word from him. Eiddileg sent another. Same thing. Silence. Dead silence.

"You can guess who was chosen to go next. That's right. Good old Doli. Anything disagreeable to be done? Any unpleasant task?"

Until now, Taran had never been aware that a frog's face could show such a look of indignation and of being much put upon.

Doli snorted, as well as he was able in his present shape. "Naturally, send for good old Doli."

"But you found who did it?" Taran asked.

"Of course I did," Doli retorted. "But I failed in the end. Look at me! Now, of all times, of all the useless things to be! Oh, if I only had my axe!

"The Fair Folk are in danger," he went on hurriedly. "Terrible danger. Yes, I learned who found our trove and stole our treasure. The same who cast this spell on me: Morda!"

"Morda?" Taran repeated, frowning. "Who is Morda? How could he have done so? Why would he dare to risk Eiddileg's wrath?"

"Why? Why?" Doli's eyes popped furiously and he began to swell up again. "Don't you understand? Morda, this foul villain of a wizard! Oh, he's shrewder than a serpent! Don't you see? He's found a way of bewitching Fair Folk! No enchanter has ever been able to cast a spell on *us*. Unheard of! Unthinkable!

"And if he's gained the power to turn us into animals—fish, frogs, no matter—we're at his mercy. He could slay us out of hand, if he chose. That's surely what happened to the way post guardian, to the messengers who vanished without a trace. It can happen to any of us. To Eiddileg himself! Not one of the Fair Folk can be safe from Morda. He's the worst threat ever to fall upon our realm."

Doli sank back exhausted by his own outburst, and the companions glanced fearfully at each other. "What his scheme is, I couldn't discover," Doli continued at last. "Oh, I tracked him to his hiding place easily enough. He lives in a sort of enclosure not too far from here. I'd gone invisible, needless to say. But it was making my ears buzz so much, worse than a pair of hornets' nests! In the darkness I thought I could chance turning visible—just for a moment, to escape that awful buzzing. Next thing I knew, there I was, as you see me now.

"Morda could have crushed me then and there. Instead, he mocked my plight. It amused him to see a helpless frog. Then he threw me down among the rocks. He savored my lingering agony more than the mercy of killing me out of hand. He was sure I'd perish in these dry hills, withering little by little to my death. And if by some chance I didn't —what difference could it make? How could a frog hope to prevail against a wizard? I crept away, trying to find water. I kept on until I could go no farther. Your cat found me then. If she hadn't, I can tell you it would have been the end of me.

"One thing Morda forgot," Doli added, "one tiny thing he overlooked: I could still speak. I myself didn't know it at the time. The shock of being turned

into a frog quite took away my voice for a while."

"Great Belin," murmured Fflewddur, "I've heard of *people* having frogs in their throats, but never . . . Forgive me, forgive me, old boy," he added quickly, as Doli glared at him. "I didn't mean to ruffle your feelings."

"Doli, tell us what we must do," Taran cried, horror-stricken at the dwarf's account. It was not Doli's plight alone that turned his blood cold; he saw clearly the fate in store for all the Fair Folk. "Lead us to Morda. We'll try to take him prisoner, or slay him if we must."

"So we shall!" exclaimed Fflewddur, drawing his sword. "I'll not have my friends turned into frogs!"

"No, no!" shouted Gurgi. "Froggies are froggies, but friends are friends!"

"Attack Morda?" Doli replied. "Are you out of your heads? You'll end up in the same pickle as me. No, you can't risk it. Eiddileg must be warned, but before that I must finish my task. Find out more of Morda's powers and how he means to use them. There's no hope of Fair Folk standing against him unless we know better what we have to deal with. Take me back to Morda's stronghold. Somehow I'll get to the bottom of his scheme. Then carry me to a way post, so I can get word to Eiddileg and spread the alarm."

A sudden spasm convulsed him; for an instant Doli seemed about to choke, then a racking sneeze nearly flung him out of the puddle. "Curse this dampness!" he sputtered. "Curse that black-hearted Morda! He's given me all the bad points of being a frog and none of the good!" Doli began coughing violently. "Blast it! Dow I ab losigg by voice! Bake haste! Bake haste! Pick be up. I'll show you the way. There's doe tibe to waste!"

The companions hurriedly mounted. With Doli clinging to his saddle horn, Taran galloped where the dwarf commanded. But the forest thickened and slowed their pace, and often in the tangle of branches they were forced to dismount and go afoot. Doli had assured them the distance was not great, but his usually unfailing sense of direction had grown confused. At times the dwarf was uncertain which path to follow, and twice the companions reined up and retraced their steps.

"Dote blade be!" snapped Doli. "I cabe over this ladd crawligg odd by belly. It's dot the sabe, seeigg it frob up here."

To make matters worse, Doli began to shake and shudder. His eyes bleared; his nostrils streamed; and even as a frog he looked altogether miserable. With constant fits of sneezing and coughing, Doli's voice grew so hoarse he could barely force out a feeble, croaking whisper, which did nothing to improve the state of his disposition or the clarity of his directions to Taran.

Until now there had been no sign of Kaw. When the companions had first hastened to follow Doli's orders, the crow had chosen this of all moments to be exasperatingly disobedient. He flapped into the woods, stubbornly refusing to heed Taran's pleas to come back. At last Taran left him behind, sure the crow would rejoin them when he saw fit; but as the companions made their way deeper into the forest, Taran had grown more anxious for the impudent bird. Thus, when they halted to set Doli on the ground—where the dwarf insisted he could better regain his bearings—Taran was too relieved to scold the crow when Kaw finally appeared. The prankster, Taran saw, had been up to his old tricks, for he bore some glittering find in his beak.

Squawking proudly, Kaw dropped the object into the surprised Taran's hands. It was the fragment of polished bone.

"What have you done?" Taran cried in dismay, as Kaw, overweeningly pleased with himself, rocked back and forth and bobbed his head.

"The jackanapes!" burst out Fflewddur. "He's gone back and rifled the coffer. I thought us well rid of that enchanted toothpick, now we've got it again.

A sour jest, you magpie!" he exclaimed, flapping his cloak at the bird, who nimbly dodged away. "A Fflam is fun-loving, but I see no joke in this at all. Throw it away," he urged Taran, "toss it into the bushes."

"I dare not, if indeed it's a thing of enchantment," Taran replied, though he felt as uneasy as the bard, and heartily wished Kaw had left the coffer undisturbed. A strange thought, vague and unformed, stirred in his mind, and he knelt, holding out the fragment to Doli. "What can this be?" he asked, after briefly telling how the sliver had first come into their hands. "Could Morda himself have hidden it?"

"Who dose?" croaked Doli. "I've dever seed eddythigg like it. But it's edchadded, you cad be sure. Keep it, id eddy case."

"Keep it?" cried the bard. "We'll have nothing but ill luck from the cursed thing. Bury it!"

Swayed by Fflewddur's vehemence yet reluctant not to follow Doli's counsel, Taran stood uncertain what to do. At last, with strong misgivings, he tucked the fragment into his jacket.

Fflewddur groaned. "Meddling! We'll only gain trouble, mark my words. A Fflam is fearless, but not when there's unknown enchantment lurking in someone's pocket."

As they pressed on Taran shortly came to believe he had decided wrongly and that Fflewddur's unhappy prediction was well-founded. Doli had taken a turn for the worse; he could gasp no more than a word or two at a time. The frog's body trembled as in the grip of a painful ague; a sickness, Taran was sure, owing to Doli's grueling crawl overland. To keep his skin from parching, the companions drenched him regularly; while the treatment, on the one hand, kept him alive, on the other it added to his misery. Under the stream of water he sneezed, choked, and sputtered. Soon he sprawled listlessly, too feeble even to be bad-tempered.

The day had waned quickly and the companions halted in a glade, for Doli had given them to understand that from now on they must travel with utmost caution. Setting the frog carefully in the folds of a dampened cloak, Taran drew Fflewddur aside and spoke hurriedly with him.

"He has no strength for his task," Taran murmured. "We dare not let him go on."

Fflewddur nodded. "I doubt he could, even if he wanted to." The bard's face, like Taran's, was drawn tightly with concern.

Taran was silent. What he must do was plain to him; yet, despite himself, he shrank from facing it. His mind groped for another, better plan, but found none, returning always to the same answer. What kept him from taking the clear course was not reluctance to help a close companion, for this he would have done gladly. Nor was it fear for his life, but terror that he might share Doli's fate; not only that his own quest would fail but that he might himself be imprisoned, hapless in some pitful creature shape, captive forever.

He knelt at Doli's side. "You must stay here. Fflewddur and Gurgi will watch over you. Tell me how I may find Morda."

CHAPTER VIII

The Wall of Thorns

Hearing this, Doli kicked weakly and croaked an incomprehensible protest, though nothing else could he do but agree to Taran's plan. With Kaw on his shoulder, Taran set off afoot through the woods. Behind him loped Gurgi, who had insisted on going with him.

After a time Taran shortened his stride and finally halted to glance around him at the forest now thick with brambles. High thorn bushes rose amid the trees in a tangled, impassable screen. Taran realized he had found what he sought. The tall bushes were no haphazard growth, but had been craftily twined into a dense barrier, a living wall nearly twice his height, bristling with spines sharper than the talons of a gwythaint. Taran drew his sword and strove to cut an opening in the thicket.

The brambles were hard as cold iron and Taran blunted both his strength and his blade against them. All he gained for his labor was a tiny hole to which he pressed his eye; he made out nothing more than a dark mound of boulders and black turf surrounded by rank weeds and burdock. What 113 first seemed the lair of a wild beast he saw to be a rambling, ill-shaped dwelling of low, squat walls roofed with sod. There was no movement, no sign of life, and he wondered if the wizard had left his fastness and the companions had come too late. The thought only put a sharper edge to his uneasiness.

"Somehow Doli forced his way in," Taran murmured, shaking his head. "But his skill is greater than mine; he must have struck on an easier passage. If we try climbing over," Taran added, "we risk being seen."

"Or caught on brambles with jabbings and stabbings!" Gurgi replied. "Oh, bold Gurgi does not like climbing walls without knowing what lies in lurkings beyond."

Taran took the crow from his shoulder. "Morda surely has his own passage: a breach in the thorns or perhaps a tunnel. Find it for us," he said urgently to Kaw. "Find it for us, old friend."

"And hasten, too," Gurgi put in. "No jokings and trickings!"

Silent as an owl, the crow flew upward, circled the barrier, then dropped out of sight. Taran and Gurgi crouched waiting in the shadows. After some while, when the sun had dipped below the trees and dusk had gathered with still no tidings from Kaw, Taran began to fear for the bird. Prankster though he was, Kaw understood the seriousness of his mission, and Taran knew it was more than whim that delayed the crow's return.

At last Taran dared wait no longer. He strode to the barrier and carefully began to climb. The branches writhed like serpents and tore viciously at his hands and face. Wherever he sought a foothold the thorns turned against him as with a will of their own. Just below, he heard Gurgi panting, as the sharp points struck through the creature's matted hair. Taran paused to catch his breath while Gurgi clambered up beside him. The top of the wall was almost within reach.

With a sudden lashing and rattling among the thorns, a slipnoose tightened around Taran's upraised arm. He shouted in alarm and in that instant glimpsed the terrified face of Gurgi as loops of finely knotted cords whipped over the creature's body. A bent sapling sprang upright, pulling the ropes with it. Taran felt himself ripped from the brambles and, dangling on the end of the strong cord, flung upward and over the barrier. Now he understood the words Doli had striven to gasp out: traps and snares. He fell, and darkness swallowed him.

A bony hand gripped his throat. In his ears rasped a voice like a dagger drawn across a stone. "Who are you?" it repeated. "Who are you?"

Taran struggled to pull away, then realized

his hands were bound behind him. Gurgi whimpered miserably. Taran's head spun. The guttering light of a candle stabbed his eyes. As his sight cleared, he saw a gaunt face the color of dry clay, eyes glittering like cold crystals deep set in a jutting brow as though at the bottom of a well. The skull was hairless, the mouth a livid scar stitched with wrinkles.

"How have you come here?" demanded Morda. "What do you seek of me?"

In the dimness Taran could make out little more than a low-ceilinged chamber and a fireless hearth filled with dead ashes. He himself had been propped in the angle of a low wall. Gurgi lay sprawled on the flagstones beside him. He glimpsed Kaw pinioned in a wicker basket set on a heavy oaken table, and he cried out to the bird.

"What then," snapped the wizard, "is this crow yours? He found one of my snares, as you did. None enters here without my knowledge. This much have you already learned. Now it is I who shall learn more of you."

"Yes, the bird is mine," Taran answered in a bold voice, deciding his only hope lay in telling as much of the truth as he dared. "He flew beyond the thicket and did not return to us. We feared some mishap and went in search of him. We journey to the Llawgadarn Mountains. You have no cause to hinder us."

"You have hindered yourselves," replied Morda, "foolish creatures without the wits of a fly. To the Llawgadarn Mountains, you say? Perhaps. Perhaps not. In the race of men is much greed and envy; but of truth, little. Your face speaks for you and calls you liar. What do you hope to hide? No matter. Your paltry store of days you call life is spun out. You shall not leave here. And yet—now you are in my hands, it may be that you shall serve me. I must ponder that. Your lives indeed may have some small use—to me, if not to yourselves."

More than the wizard's words filled Taran with horror. As he watched, unable to take his own eyes away, Taran saw that Morda's gaze was unblinking. Even in the candle flame the shriveled eyelids never closed; Morda's cold stare never wavered.

The wizard straightened and drew the grimy, threadbare robe closer about his wasted body. Taran gasped, for from Morda's withered neck hung a silver chain and crescent moon. Only one other he knew wore such an ornament: Princess Eilonwy Daughter of Angharad. Unlike Eilonwy's, the horns of this crescent held a strangely carved gem, clear as water, whose facets sparkled as though lit by an inner fire.

"The emblem of the House of Llyr!" Taran cried.

Morda started and drew back. With fingers

lean as spider's legs he clutched at the gem. "Fool,"
he hissed, "did you think to gain this from me? Is
that why you were sent? Yes, yes," he muttered, "so
it must be." His bloodless lips twitched faintly as he
fixed Taran with his unlidded eyes. "Too late. The
Princess Angharad is long dead, and all its secrets are
mine."

Taran stared at him, bewildered to hear the
name. "Angharad Daughter of Regat?" he whispered.
"Eilonwy never knew her mother's fate. But it was
you—at your hands," he burst out, "at your hands she
met her death!"

Morda said nothing for a time, seeming as one
gripped by a black dream. When he spoke, his voice
was heavy with hatred. "Think you the life or death
of one of you feeble creatures should concern me? I
have seen enough of the human kind and have
judged them for what they are: lower than beasts,
blind and witless, quarrelsome, caught up in their
own small cares. They are eaten by pride and sense-
less striving; they lie, cheat, and betray one another.
Yes, I was born among the race of men. A human!"
He spat the word scornfully. "But long have I known
it is not my destiny to be one with them, and long
have I dwelt apart from their bickerings and jeal-
ousies, their little losses and their little gains."

Deep in their shrunken sockets the wizard's
eyes glittered. "As I would not debase myself to

share their lives, neither would I share their deaths. Alone, I studied the arts of enchantment. From the ancient lore I learned the Fair Folk held certain gems hidden in their secret troves; he who possessed one gained life far longer than any mortal's mayfly span of days. None had found these treasure troves, and few had even dared to search. Yet I knew that I would learn the means to find them.

"As for her who called herself Angharad of Llyr," the wizard continued, "of a winter's night she begged refuge in my dwelling, claiming her infant daughter had been stolen, that she had journeyed long in search of her." The wizard's lips twisted. "As if her fate or the fate of a girl child mattered to me. For food and shelter she offered me the trinket she wore at her throat. I had no need to bargain; it was already mine, for too weak was she, too fevered to keep it from me if I chose to take it. She did not live out the night."

In loathing Taran turned his face away. "You took her life, as surely as if you put a dagger in her heart."

Morda's sharp, bitter laugh was like dry sticks breaking. "I did not ask her to come here. Her life was worth no more to me than the book of empty pages I found among her possessions. Though in its way the book proved to be not without some small value. In time a whining weakling found his way to me. Glew was his name, and he sought to make an enchanter of himself. Little fool! He beseeched me to sell him a magic spell, an amulet, a secret word of power. Sniveling upstart! It pleased me to teach him a lesson. I sold him the empty book and warned him not to open it or look upon it until he had traveled far from here lest the spells vanish."

"Glew!" Taran murmured. "So it was you who cheated him."

"Like all your kind," answered Morda, "his own greed and ambition cheated him, not I. His fate I know not, nor do I care to know. This much he surely learned: The arts of enchantment are not bought with gold."

"Nor stolen through heartlessness and evil, as you robbed the Princess Angharad," Taran flung back.

"Heartlessness? Evil?" said Morda. "These words are toys for creatures such as you. To me they mean nothing; my powers have borne me beyond them. The book served to make a fool taste his folly. But the jewel, the jewel served me, as all things will do at the end. The woman Angharad had told me the gem would lighten burdens and ease harsh tasks. And so it did, though years I spent in probing its secrets until I gained mastery of its use. At my command it dwindled the heaviest faggots to no more than twigs. With the gem's help I raised a wall of thorns. As my skill grew, I found the waters of a hidden spring."

The wizard's unblinking eyes glittered triumphantly. "At last," he whispered, "at last the gem led me to what I had ever sought: a Fair Folk treasure trove.

"This trove held none of the life-giving stones," Morda went on. "But what matter! If not here, then would I find them elsewhere. Now all Fair Folk treasure, mines, hidden pathways—all lay open to me.

"One of the Fair Folk watchers came upon me then. I dared not let him raise an alarm. Though none had ever stood against any of them, I did so!" cried Morda. "My jewel was more than a trinket to lighten a scullery maid's toil. I had grasped the heart of its power. At my command this Fair Folk spy turned to a sightless, creeping mole! Yes," Morda hissed, "I had gained power even beyond what I sought. Who now would disobey me when I held the means to make men into the weak, groveling creatures they truly are! Did I seek only a gem? The whole kingdom of the Fair Folk was within my grasp. And all of Prydain! It was then I understood my true destiny. The race of men at last had found its master."

"Its master?" Taran cried, aghast at Morda's words. "You are viler than those you scorn. Dare you speak of greed and envy? The power of Angharad's gem was meant to serve, not enslave. Late or soon, your life will be forfeit to your evil."

The glint in Morda's lidless eyes flickered like a serpent's tongue. "Think you so?" he answered softly.

From beyond the chamber came a shout, a sudden crashing amid the wall of thorns. Morda nodded curtly. "Another fly finds my web."

"Fflewddur!" Taran gasped as Morda strode from the chamber. He flung himself closer to Gurgi and the two tore at each other's bonds; in vain, for within a few moments the wizard returned, half-dragging a figure he trussed securely and threw to the ground beside the companions. It was, as Taran feared, the luckless bard.

"Great Belin, what's happened to you? What's happened to me?" groaned Fflewddur, stunned. "You didn't come back . . . I went to have a look—feared you'd got caught somehow in those brambles." The bard painfully shook his head. "What a jolt! My neck will never be the same."

"You shouldn't have followed us," Taran whispered. "I had no way to warn you. What of Doli?"

"Safe enough," replied Fflewddur. "Safer, at least, than we are now."

Morda had been intently watching the companions. "So it was the Fair Folk who sent you to spy on me. You are leagued with the dwarfish creature foolish enough to think he could escape me. So be it. Did I think to spare you? You will share his fate."

"Yes, Doli of the Fair Folk is our companion," Taran cried. "Unloose him from your spell. I warn you: Harm none of us. Your plan will fail, Morda. I am Taran of Caer Dallben, and we are under the protection of Dallben himself."

"Dallben," spat Morda. "Gray-bearded dotard! His powers cannot shield you now. Even Dallben will bow before me and do my bidding. As for you," he added, "I will not slay you. That would be paltry punishment. You will live—as long as you are able to live in the shapes you will soon have; live and know, during every moment of your wretched days, the cost of defying me."

Morda took the jewel and chain from about his neck and turned to Fflewddur. "Let your boldness in seeking your fellows now be cowardice. Flee at the barking of hounds or the tread of hunters. Crouch in fear at the flutter of a leaf and the passing of every shadow."

The gem flashed blindingly. Morda's hand shot forward. Taran heard Fflewddur cry out, but the bard's voice died in his throat. Gurgi screamed and Taran, horror-stricken, saw the bard no longer at his side. Kicking frantically in Morda's grasp was a dun-colored hare.

123

With a harsh laugh Morda held the animal aloft and stared scornfully at it a moment before flinging it into a wicker basket near Kaw's cage. The wizard strode to the companions and stood above Gurgi whose eyes rolled in terror and who could only gibber wordlessly.

Taran struggled against his bonds. Morda raised the gem. "This creature," said the wizard, "this half-brute serves no use. Feeble cringing beast, be weaker still, and prey to owls and serpents."

With all his strength Taran fought to break the thongs holding him. "You destroy us, Morda!" he shouted. "But your own evil will destroy you!"

Even as Taran cried these words, the gem flashed once again. Where Gurgi had lain, a gray field mouse reared on its hind legs, then fled squeaking to a corner of the chamber.

Morda turned his unlidded eyes on Taran.

CHAPTER IX

The Hand of Morda

And you," said Morda, "your doom will not be to lose yourself in forest or burrow. My plan fail? Here shall you stay prisoner and see my triumph. But what shape shall I give you? A dog whining for scraps from my table? A caged eagle eating out his heart for the freedom of the skies?"

Angharad's gem dangled from Morda's fingers. Despair choked Taran as he stared at the ornament like a bird fascinated by a serpent. He envied the wretched Gurgi and Fflewddur. A hawk's talons or a fox's jaws would shortly put a merciful finish to their days; his own would wear themselves out in the slow agony of captivity, like stone grinding against stone, until Morda was pleased to end them.

The wizard's taunts burned like drops of venom; but as Morda spoke, Taran felt a furry body press against his bound wrists. Startled, he almost cried out. His heart leaped and pounded. It was the mouse that had once been Gurgi.

Heedless of its plight, the creature had scurried noiselessly on tiny paws to the corner where Taran lay. Unseen by the wizard, the mouse flung

125

himself on Taran's bonds and with his sharp teeth began hurriedly gnawing at the thongs.

Morda, as if undecided, toyed with the jewel. Gurgi, Taran felt, was chewing desperately at the stubborn bonds; time pressed, and despite the creature's brave efforts the thongs held fast. Taran strove to draw the leather taut to aid the frantic mouse, but there was no sign of loosening, and now the wizard raised the glittering gem.

"Hold!" Taran cried. "If my fate is to be a beast, grant me this much: Let me choose which it must be."

Morda paused. "Choose?" His bloodless lips tightened in a scornful smile. "What can your wishes matter to me? And yet—perhaps it would be fitting if you chose your own prison. Speak," he commanded. "Quickly."

"At Caer Dallben," Taran began, speaking as slowly as he dared, "I was Assistant Pig-Keeper. In my charge was a white pig . . ." At his wrists one strand parted. But Gurgi's strength had begun to ebb.

"What, then," interrupted Morda, laughing harshly. "do you crave to be a swine? To wallow in mire and grub for acorns? Yes, pig-keeper, your choice indeed is fitting."

"It is my only wish," said Taran, "for it may at least remind me of a happier time."

Morda nodded. "Yes. And for that very reason, your wish will not be granted. Clever pig-
keeper," he jeered. "You have told me what you most
desire. Now I may be all the more sure you will not
have it."

"Will you not give me the shape I ask?" Taran
replied. Another strand gave way as Gurgi, fighting
weariness, redoubled his efforts. Suddenly the thongs
yielded. Taran's hands burst free. "Then," Taran
cried, "then I will keep my own!"

In the instant Taran sprang to his feet. He
snatched his blade from its sheath and lunged toward the wizard who, startled, had taken a backward
pace. Before Morda could raise the gem, with a shout
Taran drove his sword full into the wizard's breast.
He plucked the weapon free. But his shout turned to
a cry of horror and he stumbled back against the
wall.

Morda stood unharmed. His gaze never faltered. The wizard's mocking laughter rang through
the chamber.

"Foolish pig-keeper! Had I feared your sword
I would have taken it from you!"

The wizard held Angharad's gem aloft. Taran's head spun with fresh terror. In Morda's grasp
the jewel gleamed coldly. In the sudden clarity of his
fear Taran saw the sharp facets of the crystal and the
bony claw that held it. He was aware now, for the

first time, that the hand of Morda lacked a little finger; in its place was an ugly stump of scarred and withered flesh.

"Do you seek my life?" hissed Morda. "Seek, then, pig-keeper. My life is not prisoned in my body. No, it is far from here, beyond the reach of death itself!

"One last power did I gain," said the wizard. "As my jewel could shape the lives of mortal men, so could it shield my own. I have drawn out my very life, hidden it safely where none shall ever find it. Would you slay me? Your hope is useless as the sword you hold. Now, pig-keeper, suffer for your defiance. Hound or eagle would be too proud a fate. Crawl in the darkness of earth, least of all creatures, a spineless, limbless blind worm!"

Light flared in the heart of the gem. Taran's sword dropped from his grasp and he flung his arm across his face. He staggered as though a thunderbolt had struck him. Yet he did not fall. His body was still unchanged, still his own.

"What blocks my spell?" cried Morda in a terrible voice. A shadow of fear crossed his face. "As if I struggled against myself." His lidless eyes stared unbelieving at Taran, and his hand with its lacking finger gripped the gem more tightly.

In Taran's mind a strange thought raced. The
wizard's life safely hidden? Where none would find

it? Taran could not take his eyes from Morda's hand. A little finger. The coffer in the hollow tree. Slowly, terrified lest his hope betray him, Taran thrust a hand into his jacket and drew out the fragment of polished bone.

At the sight of it Morda's face seemed to crumble in decay. His jaw dropped, his lips trembled, and his voice came in a rasping whisper. "What do you hold, pig-keeper? Give it into my hands. Give it, I command you."

"It is a small thing my companions and I found," replied Taran. "How should this have worth to you, Morda? With all your power, do you covet such a trifle?"

A sickly sweat had begun to pearl on the wizard's brow. His features twitched and his voice took on a gentleness all the more horrible coming from his lips. "Bold lad to stand against me," he murmured. "I did no more than test your courage to see if you were worthy to serve me, worthy of rich rewards. You shall have gold in proof of my friendship. And in proof of yours, you shall give me—the small thing, the trifle you hold in your hand . . ."

"This worthless shard?" Taran answered. "Will you have it for a token? Then let us share it, half for me and half for you."

"'No, no, do not break it!" screamed Morda, his face turning ashen. He thrust out a skinny claw 129 and took a step toward Taran, who quickly drew back and raised the fragment of bone above his head.

"A worthless thing it is," Taran cried. "Your life, Morda! Your life I hold in my hand!"

Morda's eyes rolled madly in their wasted sockets, a violent shudder gripped him and his body quaked as though buffeted by a gale. "Yes, yes!" he cried in a voice racked with terror. "My life! Poured into my finger! With a knife I cut it from my own hand. Give! Give it back to me!"

"You set yourself above the human kind," Taran replied. "You scorned their weakness, despised their frailty, and could not see yourself as one of them. Even I, without birthright or name of my own know that if nothing else I am of the race of men."

"Kill me not!" cried Morda, writhing in anguish. "My life is yours; take it not from me!" The wizard flung himself to his knees and stretched out his trembling arms. His bloodless lips quivered as the words burst from his mouth. "Hear me! Hear me! Many secrets are mine, many enchantments. I will teach them to you. All, all!"

Morda's hands clasped and unclasped. His fingers knotted around each other and he rocked back and forth at Taran's feet. His voice had taken on a wheedling, whining tone. "I will serve you, serve you well, Master Pig-Keeper. All my knowl-edge, all my powers at your bidding." Angharad's jewel dangled from its silver chain at Morda's wrist, and he clutched it and held it up before Taran. "This! Even this!"

"The gem is not yours to give," Taran answered.

"Not mine to give, Master Pig-Keeper?" The wizard's voice grew soft and sly. "Not mine to give. But yours to take. Would you know its secret workings? I alone can tell you. Would you gain mastery of its use? Have you never dreamed of power such as this? Here, it awaits you. The race of men at your beck and call. Who would dare disobey your smallest wish? Who would not tremble in fear of your displeasure? Promise me my life, Master Pig-Keeper, and I shall promise you . . ."

"Do you bargain with enchantment you stole and corrupted?" Taran cried angrily. "Let its secrets die with you!"

At this Morda howled horribly and pressed himself almost flat on the ground. Barking sobs racked his body. "My life! Spare it! Spare it! Do not give me to death. Take the gem. Change me to the lowest crawling thing, to foulest vermin, only let me live!"

The sight of the cowering wizard turned Taran sick at heart, and for a long moment he could not speak. At last he said, "I will not kill you, Morda."

The wizard left off his frightful sobbing and lifted his head. "You will not, Master Pig-Keeper?" He crept forward and made as though to fling his arms about Taran's feet.

"I will not kill you," repeated Taran, drawing back in revulsion, "though it is in my heart to do so. Your evil is too deep for me to judge your punishment. Restore my companions," he commanded. "Then you will go prisoner with me to Dallben. He alone can give whatever justice you may hope for. Stand, wizard. Cast Angharad's jewel from you."

Morda, still crouching, slowly and reluctantly pulled the chain from his wrist. His pasty cheeks trembled as he fondled the winking gem, murmuring and muttering to himself. Suddenly he leaped upright and sprang forward. With all his might he swung the jewel at the end of its chain like a whip across Taran's face.

The sharp edges of the stone slashed Taran's forehead. With a cry he stumbled backward. Blood streamed into his eyes, blinding him. The shard of bone flew from his fingers and went spinning and skittering over the floor. Under the force of the wizard's blow, the jewel snapped from its silver chain and rolled into a corner.

In another moment the wizard was upon him growling and snarling like a mad beast. Morda's fingers clawed at Taran's throat. His yellow teeth were bared in a ghastly grin. Taran strove to tear himself from the wizard's grasp, but the frenzy of Morda's attack staggered him; he lost his footing and tumbled to earth. Uselessly he sought to break the deadly grip that stifled him. His head whirled. Through blood-filled eyes he glimpsed the wizard's face twisted in hate and fury.

"Your strength will not save you," Morda hissed. "It is no match for mine. You are weak as all your kind. Did I not warn you? My life is not in my body. Strong as death am I! So shall you die, pig-keeper!"

With sudden horror Taran knew the wizard spoke the truth; Morda's wasted arms were hard as gnarled branches, and though Taran struggled desperately, the wizard's relentless grip tightened. Taran's lungs heaved to bursting and he felt himself drowning in a black sea. Morda's features blurred; only the wizard's baleful, unlidded gaze stayed fixed.

A crash of splintering wood shattered in Taran's ears. Morda's grip suddenly slackened. Shouting in alarm and rage, the wizard leaped to his feet and spun about. His head still reeling, Taran clutched at the wall and tried to draw himself up. Llyan had burst into the chamber.

Growling fiercely, her eyes blazing gold fires, the huge cat sprang forward. Morda turned to meet her attack.

"Llyan! Beware of him!" Taran cried.

The force of Llyan's charge bore the wizard to his knees, but Morda in his unyielding strength grappled with the animal.

Llyan flung her tawny body right and left. Her powerful hind legs, their claws unsheathed, lashed vainly at the wizard, who twisted from her paws and now clung to her arching back. Yowling and spitting, the great cat tossed her head furiously, her sharp teeth flashed in her massive jaws; yet, with all her might, she could not free herself from the wizard's clutches. Taran knew even Llyan's strength would soon ebb, just as his own had failed. She had given him a moment more of life, but now Llyan herself was doomed.

The bone! Taran dropped to hands and knees seeking the shard. Nowhere did he see it. He flung aside wooden stools, upturned earthen vessels, scrabbled in the ashes of the hearth. The bone had vanished.

From behind him rose a high twittering and squeaking and he spun to see the mouse bobbing frantically on its hind legs. In its jaws the creature held the splinter of bone.

Instantly Taran caught up the polished fragment to snap it between his fingers. He gasped in dismay. The bone would not break.

134

CHAPTER X

The Broken Spell

he polished splinter was unyielding as iron. Teeth clenched and muscles trembling with his effort, Taran felt he struggled against the wizard himself. Llyan had dropped weakly to her haunches; Morda sprang free of the unconscious cat and set upon Taran once more, snatching at the fragment. The wizard's fingers locked on the middle of the shard, but Taran clung with all his strength to the ends of it. He felt the splinter bend as Morda strove to wrest it from his grasp.

Suddenly the bone snapped in two. A sound sharper than a thunderclap split Taran's ears. With a horrible scream that stabbed through the chamber, Morda toppled backward, stiffened, clawed the air, then fell to the ground like a pile of broken twigs.

That same instant the mouse vanished. Gurgi stood at Taran's side. "Kind master saves us!" he yelled, flinging his arms about Taran. "Yes, yes! Gurgi is Gurgi again! No more a mouse with shriekings and squeakings!"

In Taran's hand the sundered bone had 135

turned to gray dust, which he cast aside. Too exhausted and bewildered to speak, he could only pat Gurgi fondly and gratefully. Llyan, her deep chest heaving, climbed to her feet near Morda's broken, lifeless form. Her tawny fur still bristled furiously and her long tail looked twice its thickness. As Gurgi hastened to unloose Kaw, who jabbered at the top of his voice and beat his wings excitedly against the cage, Llyan's golden eyes darted about the chamber and from her throat rose an anxious, questioning trill.

"Great Belin!" came Fflewddur's voice, "I'm trapped as badly as before!"

Llyan loping ahead of him, Taran ran to a corner of the chamber. The basket in which Morda imprisoned the hare now held the bard, squeezed into it along with his harp and stuck fast with his long shanks dangling over one side and his arms flapping helplessly over the other.

With some difficulty Taran and Gurgi set about freeing the bard, who hardly left off stammering incoherently all the while. Fflewddur's face was ashen from fright; he blinked, shook his ragged yellow head, and heaved huge sighs of relief.

"What humiliation!" he burst out. "A Fflam! Turned into a rabbit! I felt I'd been stuffed in a woolsack! Great Belin, my nose still twitches! Never again! I told you no good comes from meddling. Though in this case, Taran old friend, it's lucky you

had that bone. Ah, ah! Easy there, that wicker's jab-
bing me. A rabbit, indeed! If I could only have got
my paws—I mean hands—on that foul Morda!"

At last out of the basket Fflewddur threw his
arms around Llyan's powerful neck. "And you, old
girl! If you hadn't come looking for us . . ." He shuddered and clapped hands to his ears. "Yes, well, let's
not think of that."

In the doorway stood a short, stocky, stoutly
booted figure dressed in russet leather; on his head a
round, close-fitting leather cap. Thumbs hooked into
his belt, he turned bright crimson eyes on each of the
companions. Instead of his customary scowl, a grin
stretched across his broad face.

"Doli!" Taran cried, first catching sight of the
dwarf. "It's you again!"

"Again?" snapped Doli, trying to make his
voice as gruff as he could. "It always was." He strode
into the chamber. For a moment he looked down at
Morda and nodded curtly. "So that's the way of it,"
he said to Taran. "I thought as much. One moment I
was a frog wrapped in a sopping wet cloak, sure all
of you had been slain, and the next—as you see
me.

"That cat of yours grew restless after a time,"
Doli went on, turning to Fflewddur. "She picked me
up, cloak and all, and went off on your trail."

"She won't let me out of her sight," replied

Fflewddur. "For which," he added, fondly rubbing Llyan's ears, "we've all to thank her."

"But how did she get through the thorns?" Taran asked. "Morda's traps . . ."

"Through?" answered Doli. "She didn't go through, she went over!" He shook his head. "In one bound! With me in her mouth! I've never seen a creature jump so high. On the other hand, I've never seen a creature like this. But what of the rest of you? What of Morda?"

"If you don't mind," Fflewddur interrupted before Taran could finish telling the dwarf of their ordeal, "I suggest leaving here immediately. A Fflam is steadfast, but there's something about enchantments, even broken ones, that tends to—ah—disturb me."

"Wait," cried Taran. "The jewel! Where is it?"

As Doli watched, puzzled, the companions hastily set about searching every corner of the chamber to no avail. Taran's concern mounted, for he was reluctant to leave the gem unfound. However, when almost ready to admit the jewel was hopelessly lost, he heard a raucous laugh above his head.

Kaw, perched on an oaken rafter, rocked back 138 and forth chuckling and squawking, delighted with himself. The jewel glittered in his beak.

"Hi, hi!" shouted Fflewddur, alarmed. "Give it up! Great Belin, you'll have us all with paws and tails again!"

After much coaxing by Taran and indignant retorts by the bard, Kaw flapped to Taran's shoulder and dropped the gem in his hand.

"Now it belongs to wise and kindly master!" Gurgi exclaimed. "Gurgi fears stone of winkings and blinkings, but not when kindly master holds it."

Doli peered at the gem as Taran held it up. "So that's how Morda meant to enslave us. I should have guessed. This comes from the Fair Folk realm," he added. "We always honored the House of Llyr and gave the stone to Princess Regat as our wedding gift. She must have handed it down to her daughter; and when Angharad vanished, the jewel vanished with her."

"And now it comes to my hands," Taran said. He cupped the gem in his palm watching the play of light in the depths of the crystal. "Morda has turned a thing of usefulness and beauty to evil ends. Whether it may ever serve its true purpose again, I do not know. To speak truth, it draws me. And frightens me, too. Its power is vast—too vast, perhaps, for any man to hold. Even if I could learn its secrets, I would not choose to do so." He smiled at

Gurgi. "Do you call me wise? At least I'm wise enough to know I'll never have wisdom enough to use it.

"Still, it may serve one purpose," Taran went on. "With this to bargain, Orddu will surely tell me who I am. Yes!" he cried. "This is a treasure she won't refuse." He stopped abruptly and paused a long moment. In his grasp lay means to gain the knowledge he craved. But his heart sank. Though he had won the gem fairly, never could he claim to be its rightful owner. It was his to bargain with no more than it had been Morda's. If Orddu accepted it, and if he should learn he was of noble birth—was a royal robe enough to hide a dishonorable deed?

He looked at Doli. "The gem is mine," Taran said. "But only mine to give, not mine to keep." Slowly he pressed the jewel into Doli's hand. "Take this. It belonged once to the Fair Folk. It belongs to them once more."

The dwarf's usual scowl softened. "You've done us a service," he answered. "Very likely the greatest service any of you mortals have done for the Fair Folk. Without your help Morda could have destroyed us all. Yes, the gem must return to our realm; it's too dangerous in other hands. You chose well. King Eiddileg will ever remember you for this. You have his thanks—and mine." Doli nodded with satisfaction and tucked the stone carefully into his jacket.

"It's made a long journey. At last it comes back to us."

"Yes, yes!" shouted Gurgi. "Take it for keepings. If kindly master will not have it, then Gurgi wants to see no more of wicked stone. Away with it, away! Do not let it turn faithful Gurgi to a mouse again!"

Taran, with a fond laugh, put a hand on Gurgi's shoulder. "Morda couldn't have changed what you truly are, any more than he could have changed Doli. Mouse though you might have seemed, you still had the heart of a lion. But what of me?" he murmured thoughtfully. "As a caged eagle, as a blind worm—could I indeed have stayed myself? Would I still have been Taran, when I scarcely know who Taran is?"

The sun had begun to climb, promising a day blue and fresh, when the companions left the wizard's fastness. The wall of thorns had fallen, shattered like the evil power that raised it, and the companions breached it without difficulty. They untethered Melynlas and Gurgi's pony, but it was not until they had gone a considerable distance that Fflewddur agreed to halt and rest. Even then, the bard appeared uncomfortable and, while Gurgi opened the wallet of food, Fflewddur sat distractedly on a hummock, meditatively fingering his ears, as though to make certain they were indeed his own.

"Rabbits!" the bard murmured. "I'll never chase another."

Taran sat apart with Doli, for there was much he had to tell and much he wanted to ask. Though Doli had regained his long frown and short patience, the occasional flicker of a grin betrayed his delight at seeing the companions again. Yet, learning of Taran's quest, Doli scowled more deeply than usual.

"The Free Commots?" said the dwarf. "We're on the best of terms with the Commot folk; they respect us and we respect them. You'll not find many in Prydain to match their stout hearts and good will, and no man lords it over his fellows because he had the luck to be born in a king's castle instead of a farmer's hut. What matters in the Free Commots is the skill in a man's hands, not the blood in his veins. But I can tell you no more than that, for we have few dealings with them. Oh, we keep a way post open here and there, just in case they might need our help. But it seldom happens. The Commot folk would rather count on themselves, and they do quite well at it. So we're more than pleased, for our own sake, as well as theirs, for we have burden enough keeping an eye on the rest of Prydain.

"As for the Mirror you speak of," Doli continued, "never heard of it. There's a *Lake* of Llunet in the Llawgadarn Mountains. More than that I can't tell you. But what have you there?" the dwarf suddenly asked, noticing Taran's battle horn for the first time. "Where did you get that?"

"Eilonwy gave it to me when I left Mona," Taran replied. "It was her pledge that we . . ." He smiled sadly. "How long ago it seems." He unslung the horn from his shoulder and handed it to Doli.

"That's Fair Folk craftsmanship," said the dwarf. "Can't mistake it." To Taran's surprise Doli squinted into one end, then the other, and raised the horn into the sunlight as though trying to peer through the mouthpiece. As Taran watched, puzzled, Doli rapped the horn sharply with his knuckles and thumped it against his knee.

"Empty!" the dwarf grumbled. "All used up. No! Hold on a moment." He pressed the bell of the horn against his ear and listened intently. "There's one left, no more than that."

"One what?" cried Taran, more than ever perplexed at Doli's words.

"One call, what did you think?" snapped Doli.

Fflewddur and Gurgi had come closer, drawn by Doli's odd behavior, and the dwarf turned to them. "This was crafted long ago, when men and Fair Folk lived in closer friendship and each was glad to help the other. The horn holds a summons to us."

"I don't understand," began Taran.

"If you'd listen to me, you would," retorted 143

Doli, handing back the battle horn. "And I mean listen. Hard." He pursed his lips and whistled three long notes of a pitch and sequence strange to Taran. "Hear that? Sound those notes on the horn—just so, mind you, and no other way. They'll bring you the nearest Fair Folk who will do whatever they can if you need help. Now, do you remember the tune?" Doli whistled the notes again.

Taran nodded and unthinkingly raised the horn to his lips.

"Not now, you clot!" shouted Doli, "Keep it in your head. I told you there was only one summons. Save it. Don't waste it. Someday, your life may hang on that call."

Taran stared in wonder at the horn. "Eilonwy herself knew nothing of this. You've done me a priceless favor, Doli."

"Favor?" snorted the dwarf. "No favor at all. The horn serves whoever happens to have it—in this case, you. I've done nothing but show you how to gain a little more use from something already yours. Favor? Humph! It's only common courtesy. But guard it well. Squander it like a fool at the first whiff of danger and you'll regret it when you really are in trouble."

"Ahem," Fflewddur whispered to Taran. "My own counsel to you is: Trust your wits, your sword, or your legs. Enchantment is enchantment, and if you'd been through what I've been through, you'd want no part of it." He frowned uneasily at the battle horn and turned away. "I'll never be the same, that's sure!" he muttered, nervously patting his ears. "Great Belin, they still feel twice as long as before!"

CHAPTER XI

Dorath

After eating, the companions stretched themselves on the turf and slept solidly the rest of the day and all that night. In the morning Doli took his leave of them. Kaw, at Doli's request, had already begun flying to the Fair Folk realm with tidings that all was well; from there, the crow would rejoin Taran.

"I'd go with you if I could," the dwarf said to Taran. "The thought of an Assistant Pig-Keeper blundering his way through the Llawgadarn Mountains makes my hair stand on end. But I dare not. Eiddileg must have the jewel safely. And who's to bring it to him? Good old Doli! Humph!"

"It saddens me to part with you," Taran said, "but you've helped me more than I could hope. The Lake of Llunet bears the same name as the Mirror and perhaps will lead me to it."

"Farewell, then," said Doli. "You've kept us all from being frogs or worse and restored a treasure to us. You'll not regret it. We Fair Folk have long memories."

146   The dwarf clasped hands with the travelers,

and pulled his leather cap tighter on his head. Doli waved one last time, and Taran watched the dwarf's stumpy figure trudging steadily across a broad meadow, growing smaller in the distance until he vanished into the skirting woods and Taran saw him no more.

Through the day the companions bore northeastward again. Taran would have been glad for Doli's guidance and keenly missed the gruff dwarf, but his spirits had never been higher; he rode eagerly, light-heartedly; the battle horn swinging from his shoulder gave him fresh courage and confidence.

"Eilonwy's gift is more precious even than I thought," he told Fflewddur. "I'm grateful to Doli for telling me its power. And more than that, for telling me of the Lake of Llunet. It's a strange thing, Fflewddur," Taran went on, "'but somehow I feel closer to the end of my quest. I believe more than ever that I'll find what I'm looking for."

"Eh? How's that?" Fflewddur answered, blinking as if he had just come awake. Though Gurgi had put all thoughts of Morda behind him, the bard seemed still shaken by his ordeal, and often lapsed into thoughtful silence when he would morosely finger his ears as though expecting them to lengthen at any moment. "Dreadful experience!" he muttered now. "A Fflam into a rabbit! What were you saying? The quest? Yes, of course."

"Smell with whiffings!" interrupted Gurgi. "Someone cooks tasty crunchings and munchings!"

"You're right," Fflewddur agreed, sniffing the air. "Oh, blast! There goes my nose twitching again!"

Taran reined Melynlas to a walk. Llyan, too, had caught the scent; her ears forward, she licked hungrily at her whiskers.

"Shall we see who it is?" asked Fflewddur. "I wouldn't say no to a hot meal—so long as it isn't rabbit!"

Taran nodded and the companions rode cautiously through the glade. He had meant to catch a first glimpse of the strangers without himself being seen; but he had gone no more than a few paces when two roughly bearded men rose from the shadows of the bushes. Taran started. The two evidently posted as guards, quickly drew their swords. One of the men whistled a bird call and stared sharply at the companions, but made no attempt to hinder them.

In the clearing Taran saw some dozen men sprawled around a cook fire, where collops of meat hung sizzling on a spit. Though armed heavily as warriors, the men wore neither the badge nor colors of any cantrev lord. Some were chewing at their food, some sharpening their blades or waxing their bowstrings. Closest to the fire, stretched at his ease, a heavy-faced man leaned on one elbow and toyed with a long dagger, which he tossed and twirled, catching it first by the hilt, then by the point. He wore a horsehide jacket whose sleeves had been ripped out; his muddy boots were thick-soled and studded with iron nails. His yellowish hair fell below his shoulders; his cold blue eyes seemed to measure the three companions with an unhurried glance.

"Welcome, lordships," he drawled as Taran dismounted. "What lucky wind blows you to the camp of Dorath?"

"I am no lord," replied Taran. "I am Taran Assistant Pig-Keeper . . ."

"No lord?" Dorath interrupted in mock surprise, a half-smile on his mouth. "If you hadn't told me, I'd never have guessed."

"These are my comrades," Taran went on, vexed that he had let Dorath make sport of him. "Gurgi. Fflewddur Fflam—he wanders as a bard of the harp, but in his own land he is a king."

"And Dorath is king wherever he rides," answered the yellow-haired man, laughing. "Now, Lord Swineherd, will you share humble fare?" With his dagger he gestured toward the roasting collops. "Eat your fill. Dorath's Company never goes short of commons. Then we'll want to know more about three such as you."

"The harper rides a strange steed, Dorath," called a man with a badly scarred face. "I wager my 149 mare could stand against the beast, no matter, for she's an evil-tempered brute and a killer born. Would it not be a merry match? What say you, Dorath? Will you have the cat show us some sport?"

"Hold your tongue, Gloff," Dorath answered, carefully eyeing Llyan. "You're a fool and always were." He pulled the meat from the spit and thrust it toward the companions. Fflewddur, having assured himself the roast was not rabbit, ate with a good will; Gurgi, as usual, needed no urging to finish his meal; and Taran was glad to swallow his own share, washed down with a mouthful of harsh-tasting wine Dorath poured from a leather flask. The sun was dropping quickly. One of the band flung more branches on the fire. Dorath stuck his dagger into the ground before him and looked up sharply at Taran.

"And so, Lord," said Dorath, "have you no traveler's tales to pass the time for my friends and me? Where do you come from? Where do you go? And why? The Hill Cantrevs are dangerous unless a man knows what he's about."

Taran did not answer immediately; Dorath's tone and the look of the men around the fire made Taran guard his words. "We journey northward— through the Llawgadarn Mountains."

Dorath grinned at him. "And where then?" he asked. "Or do you call my questions discourteous?"

"To the Lake of Llunet," Taran answered with some reluctance.

"I've heard of treasure in those parts," put in the man called Gloff. "Is that what they seek?"

"Is it indeed?" Dorath said to Taran. "Treasure?" He laughed loudly. "Small wonder you're a miser with your words!"

Taran shook his head. "If I find what I seek, it will be more to me than gold."

"So?" Dorath bent close to him. "But what would such a treasure be, Lord? Jewels? Fine-fashioned ornaments?"

"Neither," Taran answered. He hesitated, then said, "I seek my parents."

Dorath was quiet a moment. The grin did not leave his face, but when he spoke again his voice was cold. "When Dorath asks a question, he wants a truthful answer, Lord Swineherd."

Taran flushed angrily. "I have given you one. Say I have not and you call me liar."

There was a sudden silence between the two. Dorath had half-risen, his heavy face darkened. Taran's hand moved to the pommel of his sword. But in that instant a merry burst of music rose from Fflewddur's harp and the bard called out, "Gently, friends! Hear a gay tune to settle our supper!"

He leaned the beautifully curved harp against his shoulders and as his fingers danced over the strings the men around the fire clapped their hands and urged him on. Dorath settled back on the turf, but he glanced at the bard and spat into the fire.

"Have done, harper," Dorath said after a time. "Your tune jangles from that crooked pot. We'll take our rest. You'll stay with us and in the morning my Company will guide you to the Lake of Llunet."

Taran glanced at Fflewddur and caught the bard's quick frown. He rose to his feet. "We thank you for your courtesy," he said to Dorath, "but time presses and we mean to travel during the night."

"Ah, yes—so we do," Fflewddur put in, while Gurgi vigorously agreed. "As for the Lake—yes, well —we wouldn't think of putting you to the trouble. It's a long journey, far beyond your cantrev."

"Prydain is my cantrev," Dorath answered. "Have you not heard of Dorath's Company? We serve any who pay us to serve: a weak lord who craves a strong war band, or three wayfarers who need protection against the dangers of their journey. The many dangers, harper," he grimly added. "Llunet is no more than a step and a jump for my men; and I know how the land lies. Will you go safely? I ask only a little part of the treasure you seek, a small reward to your humble servants."

"We thank you," Taran said again. "It is already past nightfall and we must find our path."

"How then!" cried Dorath in a great show of

indignation. "Do you scorn my poor hospitality? You wound my feelings, lords. Is it beneath you to sleep beside the likes of us? Ah, ah, swineherd, do not insult my men. They might take it amiss."

Indeed, as Dorath spoke, an ugly grumble rose from the band, and Taran saw some of the warriors finger their swords. He stood uncertain, though well aware of the bard's discomfort. Dorath watched him closely. Two of the men had drifted quietly to the horse lines, and Taran could imagine that in the shadows they were easing their weapons from their sheaths.

"So be it," Taran said, looking Dorath squarely between the eyes. "We welcome your hospitality for the night, and tomorrow we take leave of you."

Dorath grinned. "There will be time to speak of that again. Sleep well."

"Sleep well?" muttered Fflewddur as they wrapped themselves in their cloaks and uneasily stretched out on the ground. "Great Belin, I'll not sleep a wink. I never liked the Hill Cantrevs and this is one reason more for liking them less." He glanced around him. Dorath had flung himself down near the fire; undoubtedly following his leader's order, the man named Gloff lay close by the companions. "I know of such roaming war bands," Fflewddur went on in a hushed voice. "Ruffians and looters, all of 153 them. The cantrev lord who hires their swords to fight his neighbor soon finds them at his own throat. Dorath protect us from dangers? The worst danger is Dorath himself!"

"He's sure we're after treasure," Taran whispered. "It's in his mind and he'll not believe otherwise. Lucky it is, in a way," he added ruefully. "As long as he thinks we can lead him to gold or jewels he won't kill us out of hand."

"Perhaps so, perhaps not," answered Fflewddur. "He may not cut our throats, but he might just as well decide to—ah—shall we say persuade us to tell him where the treasure is, and I fear he'd do considerably more than tweak our toes."

"I'm not sure," Taran replied. "If he meant to torture us, I think he'd have tried before this. He's put us in a tight corner and we dare not let him travel with us. Still, I don't believe Dorath is all that sure of himself. We're only three against a dozen, but don't forget Llyan. If it comes to a fight, Dorath has an excellent chance of killing us all. Yet I think he's shrewd enough to see it would cost him too dearly, perhaps most of his band and himself as well. I doubt he'll risk it unless he has to."

"I hope you're right," sighed the bard. "I'd rather not stay to find out. I'd sooner spend the night in a nest of serpents. We must get free of these villains! But how?"

Taran frowned and bit his lip. "Eilonwy's horn," he began.

"Yes, yes!" whispered Gurgi. "Oh, yes, magic horn of tootings and hootings! Help comes with rescuings! Sound it, wise master!"

"Eilonwy's horn," Taran said slowly. "Yes, that was first in my thoughts. Must I use it now? It's a precious gift, too precious to waste. If all else fails . . ." He shook his head. "Before I sound it let us try with our own strength. Sleep now," he urged. "Rest as much as you can. Before first light Gurgi can go silently to the horse lines and cut the tethers of all Dorath's steeds while Fflewddur and I try to stun the guards. Frighten the mounts, scatter them in all directions. Then . . ."

"We ride for dear life!" put in Fflewddur. He nodded. "Good. It's our best chance. Without blowing that horn of yours, I daresay it's our only chance. Dorath!" he added, cradling his harp fondly in his arms. "My tunes jangle indeed! My harp a crooked pot! That ruffian has neither ears nor eyes! A Fflam is forebearing, but when he insults my harp Dorath goes too far. Though, alas," Fflewddur admitted, "I've heard the same opinion from a few others."

While Gurgi and Fflewddur drowsed fitfully, Taran stayed wakeful and uneasy. The campfire burned to embers. He heard the heavy breathing of Dorath's men. Gloff sprawled motionless, snoring 155 atrociously. For a little time Taran closed his eyes. Had he chosen wrongly by not sounding the battle horn? He knew, painfully, that three lives hung in the balance. Doli had warned him not to squander the gift. But was the gamble too great? Should the gift be spent now, when its need was clearest? These thoughts pressed upon him heavier than the moonless night.

As the black sky began to show the first pale traces of gray, Taran silently roused Gurgi and the bard. Cautiously they made their way to the tethered steeds. Taran's heart leaped with hope. The two guards were sleeping soundly, their swords across their knees. He turned, meaning to help Gurgi cut the lines. The dark bole of an oak tree loomed, and he clung to the safety of its shadow.

A booted leg thrust out to bar Taran's way. Dorath was leaning against the tree, a dagger in his hand.

CHAPTER XII

The Wager

hat, are you so impatient to be gone, Lord Swineherd?" said Dorath, an edge of mockery in his tone. The dagger twirled in his hands and he clicked his tongue against his teeth. "Without a farewell? Without a word of thanks?" He shook his head. "This is grave discourtesy to me and to my men. Their feelings are tender. I fear you've deeply wounded them."

The men of Dorath's Company had begun to stir. In a moment of panic Taran glanced at Fflewddur and Gurgi. Gloff had climbed to his feet and held his sword lightly, almost carelessly. Taran knew the man could bring up the blade in a flash before his own weapon left its sheath. Taran's eyes darted to the horse lines. Another of Dorath's band had drifted close by the steeds, where he stood idly paring his nails with the point of a hunting knife. Taran gestured for the companions to make no move.

Dorath straightened. His eyes were cold. "Truly, do you mean to part with us? Even warned of the dangers in the hills?" He shrugged. "Never say Dorath forces hospitality on unwilling guests. Go, if that's in your head. Seek your treasure and a speedy journey to you."

"We meant you no discourtesy," Taran answered. "Bear us no ill will, for we bear you none. Farewell to you and your Company."

Much relieved, he beckoned Gurgi and the bard and turned away.

Dorath's hand gripped his shoulder. "How then!" Dorath cried, "will you go your way without settling the small matter between us?"

Taran halted, surprised, as Dorath went on.

"Why, there is payment to be reckoned, Lord Swineherd. Will you cheat me of my fee? We are poor men, Lord; too poor to give where we do not receive."

The warriors laughed harshly. Dorath's heavy face had twisted into a leering humility, which Taran found all the more fearsome by its falsity, and the man cried out in an accusing, begging tone, "You have eaten our meat and drunk our wine. All night you slept safely under our protection. Is this worth nothing to you?"

Taran stared at him in astonishment and sudden alarm. Dorath's men had come to gather near their leader. Gurgi edged closer to Taran. "Protection!" Fflewddur muttered under his breath. "Who'll protect us from Dorath? Protection? Great Belin, I'd call it robbery!"

"And there is more, Lord Swineherd," Dorath quickly continued. "The matter of payment for guiding you to the Lake of Llunet. It is no light journey for my Company; the paths are long and harsh . . ."

Taran faced the man squarely. "You have given us food, drink, and shelter," he said, his thoughts racing to seek escape from Dorath's trap. "We will pay their worth. As for your protection on our journey, we neither ask it nor want it."

"My men are willing, waiting, and ready to guide you," replied Dorath. "It is you who breaks the bargain."

"I struck no bargain with you, Dorath," Taran answered.

Dorath's eyes narrowed. "Did you not? But you will keep it nonetheless."

The two watched each other in silence for a moment. The warriors stirred restlessly. From Dorath's expression Taran could not judge whether the man indeed meant to risk battle. If he did, Taran realized coldly the companions had little chance to escape unharmed. At last he said, "What do you want from us?"

Dorath grinned. "Now you speak wisely. 159

Small scores are quickly settled. We are humble men, Lord. We ask little, far less than what our fee should be. But, for the sake of the friendship between us, Dorath will be generous. What shall you give me?" His eyes went to Taran's belt. "You carry a fair blade," he said. "It will be mine."

Taran's hand clenched on the pommel. "That you shall not have," he answered quickly. "I offer you bridles and harness from our gear, and even these we can ill afford. Dallben my master gave me this blade, the first that was truly mine and the first of my manhood. The one I love girded it on me with her own hands. No, Dorath, I do not bargain with my sword."

Dorath threw back his head and laughed. "You make much ado for a piece of iron. Your sweetling girded it to your side! Your first blade! This adds no worth. It is a fair weapon, no more. I've cast away better than that. But the look of this one suits me well enough. Give it into my hand and we are quit."

Dorath's face filled with cruel pleasure as he reached out. Sudden anger goaded Taran. Caution forgotten, he snatched the blade from its sheath and drew back a pace.

"Have a care, Dorath!" Taran cried. "Will you take my sword? It will be a costly bargain. You may not live to claim it."

160

"Nor you to keep it," Dorath answered, undisturbed. "We know each other's thoughts, swineherd. Am I fool enough to risk lives for a trinket? Are you fool enough to stop me?

"We can learn this easily," Dorath added. "To your grief or to mine. Will you try me? My Company against yours?" When Taran did not answer, Dorath continued. "My trade is to spill another's blood, not waste my own. And here the matter is easily settled. Pit one of your number against one of mine. A friendly wager, swineherd. Do you dare? The stakes? Your sword!"

Gloff had been listening all this while; his villainous face lit up and he struck his hands together. "Well spoken, Dorath! We'll see sport after all!"

"The choice is yours, swineherd," Dorath said to Taran. "Who is your champion? Will that hairy brute you call comrade stand against Gloff? They're both ill-favored enough to be well-matched. Or the harper . . ."

"The matter is between you and me, Dorath," Taran replied, "and none other."

"All the better," Dorath answered. "Do you take the wager, then? We two unarmed, win or lose, and the score paid. You have Dorath's word."

"Is your word as true as your claim?" Taran flung back. "I trust no bargain with you."

Dorath shrugged. "My men will withdraw 161

beyond the trees where they'll be no help to me, if that's what you fear. And so will yours. What say you now? Yes or no?"

"No, no!" shouted Gurgi. "Kindly master, beware!"

Taran looked long at the sword. The blade was plain, the hilt and pommel unadorned, yet even Dorath had seen the craftsmanship in its making. The day Dallben had put it in his hands shone bright in Taran's memory as the untarnished metal itself; and Eilonwy—her tart words had not hidden her blush of pride. Still, treasure it though he did, he forced himself to see the blade coldly as indeed no more than a strip of metal. Doubt rose in his heart. Win or lose, he felt unsure whether Dorath would let the companions free without a pitched battle. He nodded curtly. "So be it."

Dorath signaled to his band and Taran watched cautiously until all had made their way a good distance into the woods. At Taran's orders Fflewddur and Gurgi untethered Llyan and the two steeds and reluctantly withdrew in the opposite direction. Taran flung down his cloak and dropped Eilonwy's horn beside it. Dorath waited, a crafty glint in his eyes, as Taran slowly ungirded the scabbard and thrust the sword into the ground.

Taran stepped back. In the instant Dorath sprang upon him without warning. The force of the burly warrior's charge drove the breath from Taran's lungs and nearly felled him. Dorath grappled with him and Taran realized the man strove to seize him by the belt and hurl him to earth. Taran flung up his arms and slipped downward out of Dorath's clutches. Cursing, Dorath struck at him with a hard fist, and though Taran escaped the full weight of the blow, it glanced painfully from the side of his head. Ears ringing, Taran sought to disengage himself and regain sure footing, but Dorath pressed his attack without respite.

He dared not, Taran understood, let his heavier opponent come to grips with him, for Dorath's powerful arms could snap him in two; as the warrior plunged once more against him, Taran snatched the man's forearm and with all his strength swung Dorath head over heels to send him crashing to the ground.

But Dorath was on his feet in a flash. Taran crouched to meet the warrior's new attack. For all his weight, Dorath moved quick as a cat; he dropped to one side, spun quickly, and suddenly Taran saw the man's thick fingers gouging at his eyes. As Taran struggled to escape the blinding thrust, Dorath seized him by the hair and wrenched his head backward. The warrior's fist was raised to strike. Taran, gasping at the painful shock, flailed at the man's grinning face. Dorath's hold loosened; 163

Taran tore himself away. For an instant Dorath seemed bewildered by the rain of blows, and Taran pressed his slight advantage, darting from one side to the other, giving Dorath no chance to gain the upper hand again.

Dorath dropped suddenly to one knee and caught at Taran with an outflung arm. Striving to tear himself away, Taran felt a sharp, stinging blow to his side. He fell backward, clutching at the hurt. Dorath rose up. He gripped a short-bladed knife drawn from his boot.

"Disarm!" Taran cried. "We fight weaponless! You betray me, Dorath!"

The warrior looked down at him. "Have you learned which of us is the fool, Lord Swineherd?"

Eilonwy's horn lay within Taran's grasp and his fingers reached for it. How long, he thought hurriedly, how long before the Fair Folk might answer his call? Could he hope to keep Dorath at bay, or, at the last, could he do no more than turn and flee? He yearned desperately to sound the notes, but with an angry shout he cast aside the battle horn, snatched up his cloak for a shield, and plunged straight against Dorath.

The warrior's knife tangled in the folds of the garment. Gaining strength from his anger, Taran ripped the blade from the hand of Dorath, who staggered under the fury of the onslaught and fell to the ground. Taran followed him, seized Dorath by the shoulders, and braced his knee against the warrior's chest.

"Cut-throat!" Taran shouted through clenched teeth. "You'd have taken my life for the sake of a bit of iron."

Dorath's fingers scrabbled in the earth. His arm shot up. A handful of dirt and stones pelted against Taran's face.

"Find me now!" cried Dorath with a mighty heave. Taran clapped hands to his smarting eyes; tears streamed down his face; and he groped for the warrior who sprang away in an instant.

Taran stumbled forward on hands and knees. Dorath's heavy boot drove into his ribs. Taran cried out, then fell doubled up and panting. He strove to rise, but even the strength of his anger could not bring him to his feet. He sank down, his face pressed against the ground.

Dorath strode to the sword and plucked it from the turf. He turned to Taran. "I spare your life, swineherd," he cried scornfully. "It means naught to me and I have no wish for it. Should we meet again, it may not go as well for you."

Taran raised his head. In Dorath's eyes he saw only cold hatred that seemed to reach out to blight or shatter all it touched. "You have won nothing," Taran whispered. "What have you gained worth more to you than to me?"

"The getting pleased me, swineherd. The taking pleases me all the more." Dorath tossed the sword in the air, caught it again, then threw back his head and burst into raw laughter. He turned on his heel and strode into the forest.

Even after his strength had come back and the pain in his side had dwindled to a dull ache, Taran sat a long while on the ground before gathering up his belongings—the torn cloak, the battle horn, the empty scabbard, and setting off to join Fflewddur and Gurgi. Dorath had gone. There was no sign of him, but the laughter still rang in Taran's ears.

CHAPTER XIII

The Lost Lamb

nder fair skies and gentle weather, the companions traveled deeper into the Hill Cantrevs. Gurgi had bandaged Taran's wound and the smart of it eased more quickly than the sting of losing his sword. As for the bard, the encounter with Dorath had driven away his concern for the length of his ears; he hardly mentioned the word "rabbit," and had begun to share Taran's belief in a good ending to a hard journey. Gurgi still grumbled bitterly about the ruffians and often turned to shake an angry fist in the air. Fortunately, the companions had seen no more of the band, though Gurgi's furious grimaces might well have been enough to keep any marauders at a safe distance.

"Shameful robbings!" muttered Gurgi. "Oh, kindly master, why did you not sound helpful horn and be spared beatings and cheatings?"

"The blade meant a great deal to me," Taran answered, "but I'll find another that will serve me. As for Eilonwy's horn, once used, its power is gone beyond regaining."

167

"Oh, true!" Gurgi cried, blinking in amazement, as if such a thought had never entered his shaggy head. "'Oh, wisdom of kindly master! Will humble Gurgi's wits never grow sharper?"

"We've all wits enough to see Taran chose rightly," put in Fflewddur. "In his place I'd have done the same—ah, no, what I meant," he quickly added, glancing at the harp, "I'd have blown that horn till I was blue in the face. Ho, there! Steady, old girl!" he cried as Llyan suddenly plunged ahead. "I say, what are you after now?"

At the same time Taran heard a forlorn bleating coming from a patch of brambles. Llyan was already there, crouching playfully, her tail waving in the air and one of her paws outstretched to tug at the briars.

A white lamb was caught in the thicket and, seeing the enormous cat, bleated all the louder and struggled pitifully. While Fflewddur, strumming his harp, drew Llyan away, Taran quickly dismounted. With Gurgi's help he bent aside the brambles and picked up the terrified animal.

"The poor thing's strayed—from where?" Taran said. "I saw no farm nearby."

"Well, I suppose it knows its home better than we do," answered Fflewddur, while Gurgi eyed the

lost animal and delightedly patted the creature's

fleecy head. "All we can do is let it go to find its own path."

"The lamb is mine," called a stern voice.

Surprised, Taran turned to see a tall, broadshouldered man making his way with great difficulty down the rocky slope. Gray streaked his hair and beard, scars creased his wide brow, and his dark eyes watched the companions intently as he toiled over the jutting stones. Unarmed save for a long hunting knife in his leather belt, he wore the rude garb of a herdsman; his cloak was rolled and slung over his back; his jacket was tattered at the edges, begrimed and threadbare. What Taran had first taken to be a staff or shepherd's crook he now saw to be a roughly fashioned crutch. The man's right leg was badly lamed.

"The lamb is mine," the herdsman said again.

"Why, then it is yours to claim," Taran answered, handing the animal to him.

The lamb ceased its frightened bleating and nestled comfortably against the shoulder of the herdsman, whose frown of distrust turned to surprise, as if he had fully expected to be obliged to fight for possession of the stray. "My thanks to you," he said after a moment, then added, "I am Craddoc Son of Custennin."

"Well met," Taran said, "and now farewell. Your lamb is safe and we have far to go."

Craddoc, taking a firm grip on his crutch, turned to climb the slope, and had gone but little distance when Taran saw the man stumble and lose his footing. Under his burden Craddoc faltered and dropped to one knee. Taran strode quickly to him and held out his hands.

"If the way to your sheepfold is as stubborn as the ones we've traveled," Taran said, "let us help you on your path."

"No need!" the herdsman gruffly cried. "Do you think me so crippled I must borrow strength from others?" When he saw that Taran still offered his hands, Craddoc's expression softened. "Forgive me," said the herdsman. "You spoke in good heart. It was I who took your words ill. I am unused to company or courtesy in these hills. You've done me one service," he went on, as Taran helped him to his feet. "Now do me another: Share my hospitality." He grinned. "Though it will be small payment for saving my lamb."

As Fflewddur led the mounts and Gurgi happily bore the lamb in his arms, Taran walked close by the herdsman who, after his first reluctance, was willing now to lean on Taran's shoulder as the path steepened and twisted upward before dropping into a deep vale among the hills.

The farmstead Taran saw to be a tumbledown cottage, whose walls of stone, delved from the surrounding fields, had partly fallen away. Half-a-dozen ill-shorn sheep grazed over the sparse pasture. A rusted plow, a broken-handled mattock, and a scant number of other implements lay in an open-fronted shed. In the midst of the high summits, hemmed in closely by thorny brush and scrub, the farm stood lorn and desolate, yet clung doggedly to its patch of bare ground like a surviving warrior flinging his last, lone defiance against a pressing ring of enemies.

Craddoc, with a gesture almost of shyness and embarrassment, beckoned the companions to enter. Within, the cottage showed scarcely more cheer than the harsh land around it. There were signs Craddoc had sought to repair his fireplace and broken hearthstone, to mend his roof and chink up the crannies in the wall, but Taran saw the herdsman's labor had gone unfinished. In a corner a spinning wheel betokened a woman's tasks; but if this were so, her hand had ceased to guide it long since.

"Well, friend herdsman," Fflewddur remarked heartily, seating himself on a wooden bench by a narrow trestle table, "you're a bold man to dwell in these forsaken parts. Snug it is," he quickly added, "very snug but—ah, well—rather out of the way."

"It is mine," Craddoc answered, and his eyes flashed with pride. Fflewddur's words seemed to stir him, and he bent forward, one hand gripping his crutch and the other clenched upon the table. "I 171 have stood against those who would have taken it from me; and if I must, so shall I do again."

"Why, indeed I've no doubt of that," replied Fflewddur. "No offense, friend, but I might say I'm a little surprised anyone would fancy taking it from you in the first place."

Craddoc did not answer for a time. Then he said, "The land was fairer than you see it now. Here we lived among ourselves, untroubled and at peace, until certain lords strove to claim our holdings for themselves. But those of us who prized our freedom banded together against them. Hotly fought was the battle and much was destroyed. Yet we turned them back." Craddoc's face was grim. "At high cost to us. Our dead were many, and my closest friends among them. And I," he glanced at his crutch, "I gained this."

"What of the others?" Taran asked.

"In time, one by one, they quit their homes," Craddoc replied. "The land was no longer worth the keeping or the taking. They made their way to other cantrevs. In despair they took service as warriors or swallowed their pride and hopes and labored for any who would give them bed and board."

"Yet you stayed," Taran said. "In a ruined land? Why so?"

Craddoc lifted his head. "To be free," he answered curtly. "To be my own man. Freedom was what I sought. I had found it here, and I had won it."

"You are luckier than I, friend herdsman," Taran answered. "I have not yet found what I seek."

When Craddoc glanced inquiringly at him, Taran told of his quest. The herdsman listened intently, saying no word. But as Taran spoke, a strange expression came upon Craddoc's face, as though the herdsman strove against disbelief and sought to reach out beyond his own wonder.

When Taran finished, Craddoc seemed about to speak. But he hesitated, then set the crutch under his arm, and rose abruptly, murmuring that he must see to his sheep. As he hobbled out, Gurgi trotted after him to gaze with pleasure at the gentle animals.

The day had grown shadowed. Taran and Fflewddur sat quietly at the table. "I pity the herdsman as much as I admire him," Taran said. "He fought to win one battle only to lose another. His own land is his worst foe now, and little can he do against it."

"I'm afraid you're right," agreed the bard. "If the weeds and brambles press him any closer," he wryly added, "he must soon graze his sheep on the turf of his rooftop."

"I would help him if I could," Taran replied. "Alas, he needs more than I can give."

When the herdsman came back Taran made

ready to take his leave. Craddoc, however, urged the companions to stay. Taran hesitated. Though anxious to be gone, he well knew that Fflewddur disliked traveling at night; as for the herdsman, his eyes more than his words bespoke his eagerness, and at last Taran agreed.

Craddoc's provisions being scant, the companions shared out the food from Gurgi's wallet. The herdsman ate silently. When he had done, he cast a few dry, thorny branches on the small fire, watched them flare and crackle, then turned his gaze on Taran.

"A lamb of my flock strayed and was found again," Craddoc said. "But another once was lost and never found." The herdsman spoke slowly and with great effort, as though the words came from his lips at some painful cost. "Long past, when all had left the valley, my wife urged that we, too, should do the same. She was to bear our child; in this place she saw naught but hardship and desolation, and it was for the sake of our unborn that she pleaded."

Craddoc bowed his head. "But this I would not do. As often as she besought me, as often I refused. In time the child was born. Our son. The infant lived; his mother died. My heart broke, for it was as if I myself had slain her.

"Her last wish," Craddoc said, his voice heavy with grief, "was that I take the child from here." His weathered features tightened. "Even that wish I did not heed. No," he added, "to my mind, I had paid in blood, and more than blood, for my freedom. I would not give it up."

The herdsman was silent a while. Then he said, "Alone I sought to raise the child. But it was beyond my skill. A sturdy boy he was, yet in less than a year I saw him sicken. Only then did I understand his mother had spoken wisely, and I, like a proud fool, had not listened. At last I was willing to quit this valley.

"Too late was my choice," Craddoc said. "I knew the babe could not live out the journey. Nor could he live out another winter here. He was the lamb of my heart, already given to death.

"But on a certain day," Craddoc went on, "a wayfarer came by chance to my door. A man of deep knowledge he was and of many secret healing arts. In his hands alone the child could live. This he told me, and I knew he spoke the truth. He pitied the infant and offered to raise him for me. Grateful was I for his kindness as I put the child in his arms.

"He went his way then, and my son with him. No more did I see or hear of either, as the years passed, and often did I fear both had surely perished in the hills. Yet, I still hoped, for the stranger vowed by every oath my son one day would return to me."

The herdsman looked closely at Taran. "The name of the wayfarer was Dallben."

In the fireplace a thorny branch split and crackled. Craddoc said no more, but his eyes never left Taran's face. Fflewddur and Gurgi stared wordlessly. Slowly Taran rose to his feet. He felt himself trembling, for an instant feared his legs would give way under him, and he put a hand to the edge of the trestle table. He could neither think nor speak. He saw only Craddoc silently watching him, and this man he had met as a stranger now seemed a stranger all the more. Taran's lips moved without sound, until at last the words came brokenly and he heard his voice as though it were another's.

"Do you say," Taran whispered, "do you say then, you are father to me?"

"The promise has been kept," Craddoc answered quietly. "My son has come back."

CHAPTER XIV

The End of Summer

t was near dawn. The fire in the hearth had long since burned out. Taran rose silently. He had slept only fitfully, his head crowded with so many thoughts he could not sort one from another: Fflewddur's cry of astonishment, Gurgi's joyful yelps, Craddoc's embrace of welcome to a son he had scarcely seen, and Taran's bewildered embrace to a father he had never known. There had been harp playing and singing. Fflewddur had never been in better voice or spirits, and the herdsman's cottage had surely never rung with so much merriment; yet Taran and Craddoc had been more quiet than gay, as if striving to sense each other's mind and heart. At last, all had slept.

Taran stepped to the door. The sheep were silent in their fold. The mountain air was chill. Dew glistened, a net of cold silver on the sparse pasture, and the stones twinkled like stars fallen to earth. Taran shivered and drew his cloak about him. He stood a while in the dooryard before he sensed he was not alone. Fflewddur moved to join him.

"Couldn't sleep, eh?" Fflewddur said cheerily. "Neither could I. Too excited. Didn't close my eyes for three winks—ah, yes, well—perhaps a few more than that. Great Belin, but it's been a day and a half! It's not everyone who finds his long-lost father sitting out in the middle of nowhere. Taran, my friend, your search is ended; and ended well. We're spared a journey to the Lake of Llunet—I don't mind telling you I'm just as pleased. Now we must set our plans. I say we should ride north to the Fair Folk realm and get hold of good old Doli; then, on to my kingdom for some feasting and revelry. And I suppose you'll want to sail to Mona and tell Eilonwy the good news. So be it! Now your quest is over, you're free as a bird!"

"Free as the caged eagle that Morda would have made me!" Taran cried. "This valley will destroy Craddoc if he stays alone even a little longer. His burden is too great. I honor him for trying to bear it. Indeed, I honor him for that, and nothing else. His deeds cost my mother her life, and nearly cost me mine. Can any son love such a father? Yet as long as Craddoc lives, I am bound to him by ties of blood—if truly his blood runs in my veins."

"If?" replied Fflewddur. He frowned and looked closely at Taran. "You say *if,* as though you doubted . . ."

"Craddoc speaks truth when he says he is my

father," Taran answered. "It is I who do not believe him."

"How's that again?" asked Fflewddur. "You know he's your father and doubt it at the same time? Now you really baffle me."

"Fflewddur, can you not see?" Taran spoke slowly and painfully. "I don't believe him, because I don't *want* to believe him. In my heart, secretly, I had always dreamed, even as a child, that—that I might be of noble lineage."

Fflewddur nodded. "Yes, I take your meaning." He sighed. "Alas, there's no choosing one's kinsmen."

"Now," Taran said, "my dream is no more than a dream, and I must give it up."

"His tale rings true," answered the bard. "But if there's doubt in your heart, what shall you do? Ah, that rascal Kaw! If he were only here we could send him with word to Dallben. But I doubt he'll find us in this dreary wasteland."

"Wasteland?" said the voice of Craddoc.

The herdsman stood in the doorway. Taran quickly turned, ashamed of his own words and wondering how many of them Craddoc had overheard. But if the man had been there longer than a moment, he gave no sign of it. Instead, his weather-beaten face smiled as he hobbled to the companions. Gurgi followed behind him.

"Wasteland you see it now," Craddoc said, "but soon as fair as ever it was." He set a hand proudly on Taran's shoulder. "My son and I. We will make it so."

"I had thought," Taran began slowly, "I had hoped you would return with us to Caer Dallben. Coll and Dallben will welcome you. The farm is rich, and can be richer still if you help us with your labor. Here, the land may be worn out past restoring."

"How then?" Craddoc answered, his features growing stern. "Leave my land? To be another's servant? Now? When there is hope for us at last?" His eyes filled with pain as he looked at Taran. "My son," he said quietly, "you do not say all that is in your heart. Nor have I said all that is in mine. My happiness blinded me to the truth. Your life has been too long apart from me. Caer Dallben is your home, more than this may ever be, this wasteland, this fallow ground—and the master of it a cripple."

The herdsman had not raised his voice, but the words echoed in Taran's ears. Craddoc's face had gone hard as stone and a terrible pride flamed in his eyes. "I cannot ask you to share this, nor beg duty from a son who is a stranger to me. We have met. We shall part, if that is your wish. Go your own path. I do not keep you from it."

Before Taran could answer, Craddoc turned 180 and made his way to the sheepfold.

"What must I do?" Taran cried in dismay to the bard.

Fflewddur shook his head. "He'll not leave here, that's for certain. It's easy enough to see where your stubborn streak comes from. No, he won't budge. But if you'd set your mind at rest, then you yourself might go to Caer Dallben. Find out the truth from Dallben. He alone can tell you."

"Winter would be upon us before I could return," Taran answered. He gazed at the harsh land and desolate cottage. "My—my father is at the end of his strength. The tasks are long. They must begin now, and be done before the first snowfall."

He said no more for a time. Fflewddur waited silently; Gurgi was quiet, his brow wrinkled with concern. Taran looked at the two and his heart ached. "Hear me well, my friends," he said slowly. "Fflewddur, if you are willing, ride to Caer Dallben. Tell that my search is ended and how this has come about. As for me, my place must be here."

"Great Belin, you mean to stay in this wilderness?" Fflewddur cried. "Even though you doubt . . . ?"

Taran nodded. "My doubts may be of my own making. One way or another, I pray you send word speedily to me. But Eilonwy must be told nothing of this, only that my quest is over, my father found." His voice faltered. "Craddoc needs my help; his livelihood and his life depend on it, and I will not with-

181

hold it from him. But to have Eilonwy know I am a herdsman's son . . . No!" he burst out. "That would be more than I could bear. Bid her my farewell. She and I must never meet again. It were better the Princess forget the shepherd boy, better that all of you forget me."

He turned to Gurgi. "And you, best of good friends, ride with Fflewddur. If my place is here, yours must be in a happier one."

"Kindly master!" Gurgi shouted, flinging his arms desperately about Taran. "Gurgi stays! So he promised!"

"Call me master no more!" Taran bitterly flung back. "No master am I, but a low-born churl. Do you long for wisdom? You will not find it here with me. Take your freedom. This valley is no beginning but an ending."

"No, no! Gurgi does not listen!" shouted Gurgi, clapping his hands over his ears. He threw himself flat on the ground and lay stiff as a poker. "He does not go from side of kindly master. No, no! Not with pullings and pushings! Not with naggings and draggings!"

"So be it," Taran said at last, seeing nothing else would sway the determined creature.

When Craddoc returned, Taran told him only that he and his companion would stay, and that

Fflewddur could no longer delay his own journey.

When Llyan was ready to travel, Taran put his arms about the cat's mighty shoulders and pressed his cheek into her deep fur as she mewed unhappily. Silently, he and Fflewddur clasped hands, and he watched while the bard, with many a backward glance, rode slowly from the valley.

Leaving Melynlas and the pony tethered in the shed, Taran and Gurgi bore the saddlebags holding their few possessions into the tumbledown cottage. Taran stood a moment, looking at the crumbling walls of the narrow chamber, the dead fire and broken hearthstone. From the pasture Craddoc was calling to him.

"And so," Taran murmured, "and so have we come home."

In the weeks that followed, Taran believed he could have fared no worse had Morda done as he had threatened. Tall gray summits rose about him like the unyielding bars of a cage. Prisoner, he sought freedom from his memories in the harsh toil of the long days. There was much to be done, indeed there was all to be done; the land to clear, the cottage to repair, the sheep to tend. At first he had dreaded the dawns that brought him, weary as if he had not slept, from the straw pallet by the hearth to the seemingly endless labor awaiting him; but soon 183 he rediscovered, as Coll had told him long ago, that he could force himself to plunge into it as into an icy stream, and find refreshment even in his exhaustion.

With Gurgi and Craddoc, he strained and sweated to uproot boulders from the field and haul them to the cottage, where they would later serve to mend the walls. The spring where the sheep watered had dwindled to a slow trickle. Taran saw a way to unblock it, shore up the damp ground, and dig a channel which he lined with flat stones. As the sparkling stream rushed into its new course, Taran, forgetting all else, knelt and drank of it from his cupped hands. The cool draught filled him with wonder, as though never had he tasted water until now.

One day the three set about burning away the overgrowth and thorns. Taran's portion of the field took flame too slowly and he pressed his way to thrust his torch deeper amid the brambles. As he did, a sudden gust of wind turned the fire against him. Quickly he drew back, but the thorns caught at his jacket; he stumbled and fell, crying out as the flames rose in a scarlet wave.

Gurgi, at some distance, heard the shout. Craddoc, seeing Taran's plight, swung about on his crutch, and even before Gurgi could reach him, flung himself to Taran's side. The herdsman dropped to the ground, and, shielding Taran with his body, seized him by the belt and dragged him clear. Where

Taran had been trapped, the flaming thorns roared and crackled.

The herdsman, gasping from the effort, climbed painfully to his feet.

Though Taran was unscathed, the fire had seared Craddoc's brow and hands. But the herdsman grinned, clapped Taran on the shoulder, saying with rough affection, "I've not found a son only to lose him," and with no more ado went back to his work.

"My thanks to you," Taran called. But in his voice there was as much bitterness as gratitude, for the man who had saved his life was the same man who had broken it.

Thus it was in the days that followed. When a sheep sickened, Craddoc cared for it with an unexpected tenderness that went to Taran's heart. Yet Craddoc it was who had torn asunder Taran's dream of noble birth and destroyed every hope he had cherished for Eilonwy. When danger threatened the flock, Craddoc turned fierce as a wolf, heedless of his own safety with a courage Taran could only admire. Yet this man held him prisoner, in fetters of blood right. Craddoc would touch no food until Taran and Gurgi had their fill, and often went hungry as a result, all the while insisting his appetite was dull. Yet the gift stuck in Taran's throat, and he scorned the generosity he would have honored in any other man.

"Are there two herdsman in this valley?" Taran cried to himself. "One I can only love, and one I can only hate?"

So passed the summer. To forget the anguish of his divided heart, Taran labored for the sake of the labor itself. Many tasks were still to be done, and the flock always to be tended. Until now Craddoc had been hard-pressed to keep the new lambs from straying and, as the sheep roved farther afield seeking better pasture, to gather all into the fold at evening. Gurgi pleaded to be given charge of them, and the flock seemed as pleased as he was. He gamboled happily with the lambs, clucked and fussed over the ewes, and even the ancient, bad-tempered ram turned gentle in his presence. As the days grew cooler Craddoc gave him a jacket of unshorn fleece, and as Gurgi moved among his charges Taran could hardly distinguish the shaggy creature bundled in his wooly garb from the rest of the flock. Often Taran came upon him sitting on a boulder, the sheep in an admiring circle around their guardian. They followed him everywhere and would even have trotted after him into the cottage. Marching at the head of the flock, Gurgi looked as proud as a war leader.

"See with lookings!" Gurgi shouted. "See them heed Gurgi with bleatings! Is kindly master Assistant

Pig-Keeper? Then bold, clever Gurgi now is Assistant Sheep-Keeper!"

But Taran's eyes still turned beyond the barrier of the hills. At the end of each day he scanned the passes for a sign of Fflewddur and the clouds for a glimpse of Kaw. The crow, he feared, had flown to the Lake of Llunet; not finding the companions there, Kaw might still be waiting or, impatient, be seeking them elsewhere. As for the bard, Taran sensed more than ever that Fflewddur would not return; and as the days shortened and autumn drew closer, he gave up his vigil and looked no longer at the sky.

CHAPTER XV

The Open Cage

Throughout summer and fall the three had worked unstintingly to finish the cottage, their only refuge against the oncoming winter. Now, as the first snow whirled from the heavy sky to powder the crags with dry, white flakes, it was done. The walls of new stone rose firm and solid; the roof had been thatched anew and tightly chinked against wind and weather. Within, a fire cheerily blazed in the new hearth. The wooden benches had been mended; the door no longer sagged on broken hinges. Though Craddoc had given himself unsparingly to the toil, the cottage for the most part was Taran's labor. The rusted tools, sharpened and refurbished, served him to make what other tools he needed. The planning as well as the doing had been his, and as he stood in the dooryard, the fine snow clinging like chaff to his uncropped hair, it was not without pride that he watched the smoke rising from the rebuilt chimney.

Craddoc had come to stand beside him, and the herdsman put a hand fondly on Taran's shoulder.

For a time neither spoke, but at last Craddoc said,

"For all the years I strove to keep what was mine, it is mine no longer." His bearded face furrowed in a smile. "Ours," he said.

Taran nodded, but made no further answer.

Since the winter tasks were short, the brief days seemed longer. Evenings by the fire, to while away the time, Craddoc told of his youth, of his settling in the valley. As the herdsman spoke of his hopes and hardships, Taran's admiration quickened, and for the first time he saw Craddoc as a man who had been not unlike himself.

Thus, at Craddoc's urging, Taran was willing to tell of his days at Caer Dallben and all that had befallen him. Craddoc's face brightened with fatherly pride as he heard of these adventures. Yet, often Taran would stop in the midst of his recounting when memories of Eilonwy and all his life long past would surge suddenly and break upon him like a wave. Then would he break off abruptly, turn his face away, and stare at the fire. Those times Craddoc pressed him to speak no further.

A bond of affection, born of their common toil, had grown among all three. Craddoc never failed to treat Gurgi with much kindness and gentleness, and the creature, more than ever pleased with his duties as shepherd, was well content. But once, at the beginning of winter, Craddoc spoke apart with Taran, saying, "Since the day you came to dwell here 189

I have called you my son, yet never have you called me father."

Taran bit his lips. At one time, he had yearned to shout aloud his bitterness, to fling it angrily in the herdsman's face. It still tormented him, but now he could not bring himself to wound the feelings of one he scorned as a father yet honored as a man.

Seeing Taran's distress, Craddoc nodded briefly. "Perhaps," he said, "perhaps one day you shall."

Snow turned the gray summits glistening white, yet the tall peaks Taran once had seen as bars now shielded the valley from the brunt of the storms, and against the wolf-wind howling through the ice-bound passes the cottage stood fast. Late of an afternoon, when Craddoc and Gurgi had gone to see to the flock, the gale sharpened and Taran set about stretching a heavier sheepskin across the narrow window.

He had only begun when the door was flung open as though ripped from its hinges. Shouting frantically, Gurgi burst into the cottage.

"Help, oh help! Kindly master, come with hastenings!" Gurgi's face was pale as ashes, his hands shook violently as he clutched at Taran's arm. "Master, master, follow Gurgi! Quickly, oh, quickly!"

Taran dropped the sheepskin, hurriedly donned a fleece jacket and, as Gurgi moaned and wrung his hands, snatched up a cloak and raced through the open door.

Outside, the wind caught at him and nearly flung him backward. Gurgi pressed on, wildly waving his arms. Taran bent forward against the gale and ran beside his desperate companion, stumbling across the snow-swept field. At the edge of the pasture they had cleared during the summer the land fell sharply away into stony slopes, and he followed close behind Gurgi as the creature scrambled past a rocky draw, then along a twisting path where he soon halted.

Taran gasped in dismay as Gurgi, whimpering fearfully, pointed downward. A narrow ledge jutted from the sheer side of the gorge. A figure, arms outflung, lay motionless, one leg twisted under his body, partly covered with fallen stones. It was Craddoc.

"Gone with stumblings!" Gurgi moaned. "Oh, miserable Gurgi could not save him from slippings!" He clapped his hands to his head. "Too late! Too late for helpings!"

Taran's head spun with shock; grief struck him like a sword. But then, beyond his will, terrifying in its sudden onrush, a wild sense of freedom flooded him as though rising from the most hidden depths of his heart. In one dizzying glance he seemed to see his cage of stone crumble.

The still form on the ledge stirred painfully and lifted an arm.

"He lives!" Taran cried.

"Oh, master! How do we save him?" Gurgi wailed. "Terrible crags are steep! Even bold Gurgi fears to climb down!"

"Is there no way?" Taran exclaimed. "He's badly hurt; dying, perhaps. We cannot leave him." He pressed his fists to his reeling forehead. "Even if we could make our way to him, how should we bear him up? And if we fail—not one life lost but three."

His hands were shaking. It was not despair that filled him, but terror, black terror at the thoughts whispering in his mind. Was there the slimmest hope of saving the stricken herdsman? If not, even Prince Gwydion would not reproach Taran's decision. Nor would any man. Instead, they would grieve with him at his loss. Free of his burden, free of the valley, the door of his cage opened wide, and all his life awaited him; Eilonwy, Caer Dallben. He seemed to hear his own voice speak these words, and he listened in shame and horror.

Then, as if his heart would burst with it, he cried out in terrible rage, "What man am I?"

Blind with fury at himself, he sprang down

the slope and clawed for a handhold amid the ice-covered stones, while Gurgi, panting fearfully, clambered after him. Taran's numbed fingers clutched vainly at an outcropping as a rock gave way beneath his feet. Downward he pitched, and cried out as a jagged stone drove against his chest. Black suns burst in his head and he choked with pain. Above, Gurgi was sliding down in a shower of ice and pebbles. Taran's heart pounded. He was on the ledge. Craddoc lay within arm's reach.

Taran crawled to his side. Blood streamed down Craddoc's brow as the herdsman struggled to raise his head. "Son, son," he gasped, "you have lost your life for me."

"Not so," Taran answered. "Don't try to move. We'll find a way to bring you to safety." He raised himself to his knees. Craddoc was even more grievously hurt than Taran had feared. Carefully he lifted away the heavy stones and shale that pressed against the herdsman, and gently drew him closer to the protecting face of the cliff.

Gurgi had dropped to the ledge and scurried to join Taran. "Master, master," he cried, "Gurgi sees a pathway upward. But it is steep, oh, steep, with dangers of hurtful stumblings and tumblings!"

Taran glanced at where the creature pointed. Amid the rocks and snow-filled crevices he could make out a narrow passageway, free of ice. Yet, as

Gurgi had warned, it rose nearly straight up. One man at a time could scale it; but what of two, burdened with a third? He gritted his teeth. The sharp stone had wounded him sorely as a blade, and each breath he drew filled his lungs with fire. He gestured for Gurgi to lay hold of Craddoc's legs, while he edged unsteadily along the sheer drop and slid his hands under the herdsman's shoulders. As gently as the companions strove to lift him, Craddoc cried out in agony, and they were forced to halt, fearful their efforts would do him further harm.

A wind had risen, screaming through the valley, lashing at the companions and nearly tearing them from the ledge. Once more they struggled to bear Craddoc to the upward passage, and once more fell back as the gale battered them. The early twilight had begun deepening and shadows filled the gorge. The face of the cliff wavered before Taran's eyes. His legs trembled as he forced himself again to lift the herdsman.

"Leave me," Craddoc murmured hoarsely. "Leave me. You waste your own strength."

"Leave you?" Taran burst out. "What son forsakes his own flesh and blood?"

Hearing this, Craddoc smiled for an instant, then his face drew taut in anguish. "Save yourselves," he whispered.

194   "You are my father," Taran replied. "I stay."

"No!" the herdsman cried out with all his strength. "Do as I ask, and go from here. Heed me now, or it will be too late. The duty of kinship? You owe me none. No bond of blood holds you."

"How then?" Taran gasped, staring wildly at the herdsman. His head spun and he clutched at the ledge. "How then? Do you tell me I am not your son?"

Craddoc looked at him a moment, his eyes unwavering. "Never have I been false to any man. Save once. To you."

"A lie?" Taran stammered in dismay. "Did you lie to me then—or do you lie to me now?"

"Half-truth is worse than lie," Craddoc answered brokenly. "Hear me. Hear this part of the truth. Yes, long past, as he journeyed through Prydain, Dallben sheltered with me. But of what he sought he never spoke."

"The child," Taran cried. "There was none?"

"There was," Craddoc answered. "A son. Our first born, even as I told you. He did not live beyond the day of his birth. His mother died with him," he murmured. "And you—I needed your strength to keep what remained to me. I saw no other way. Even as I spoke the lie, I was ashamed, then more ashamed to speak the truth. When your companion left, I could only hope that you would follow with him, and gave you freedom so to do. You chose to stay.

"But this, as well, is true," Craddoc said hur- 195

riedly. "At first I leaned upon you as on my crutch, because you served my need, but no father came to love a son more dearly."

Taran's head sank to his breast. He could not speak, and his tears blinded him.

Craddoc, who had half-raised himself, fell back to the stones of the ledge. "Go from here," he murmured.

Taran's hand dropped to his side. His fingers touched the rim of the battle horn. With a sudden cry he straightened. Eilonwy's horn! Unthinking, he had slung it about his shoulder when he had run from the cottage. Hastily he drew it from beneath his cloak. The summons to the Fair Folk, the call he had treasured! It alone could save Craddoc. He stumbled to his feet. The ledge seemed to sway beneath him. The notes Doli had taught him blurred in his mind and he strove desperately to recall them. Suddenly they rang once more in his memory.

He raised the horn to his lips. The notes sprang loud and clear and even before the signal faded, the wind caught them and seemed to fling the call through all the valley, where it returned in echo after echo. Then whirling shadows engulfed him and Taran dropped to the ledge.

How long they clung there he did not know; whether moments or hours, he was only dimly aware
of strong hands bearing him up, of a rope lashed

about his waist. He glimpsed vaguely, as between the flickering of a dark flame, the broad faces of dwarfish mountaineers, whose number he could not judge.

When next he opened his eyes he was in the cottage, the fire blazing, Gurgi beside him. Taran started up. Pain seared his chest, which he saw had been carefully bandaged.

"The signal!" he murmured feebly. "It was answered . . ."

"Yes, yes!" Gurgi cried. "Fair Folk save us with mighty haulings and heavings! They bind up kindly master's hurtful wounds and leave healing herbs for all that is needful!"

"The summons," Taran began. "Good old Doli. He warned me not to waste it. For Craddoc's sake, I'm glad I kept it as long as I did. Craddoc—where is he? How does he fare?" He stopped suddenly.

Gurgi was looking at him silently. The creature's face wrinkled miserably and tears stood in his eyes as he bowed his shaggy head.

Taran fell back. His own cry of anguish rang in his ears. Beyond that was only darkness.

CHAPTER XVI

Taran Wanderer

ever came, sweeping over him, a blazing forest through which he staggered endlessly; tossing on the straw pallet, he knew neither day nor night. Often there were dream faces half-glimpsed, half-recognized, of Eilonwy, of his companions, of all whom he had loved; yet they slipped away from him, shifting and changing like wind-driven clouds, or were swallowed by nightmares that made him cry out in terror. Later, he seemed to see Fflewddur, but the bard had turned gaunt, hollow-eyed, his yellow hair matted on his forehead, his mouth pinched and his long nose thin as a blade. His garments hung ragged and stained. Kaw perched on his shoulder and croaked, "Taran, Taran!"

"Yes, well, indeed it's about time you're waking up," said Fflewddur, grinning at him. Beside the bard, Gurgi squatted on a wooden stool and peered at him anxiously.

Taran rubbed his eyes, unsure whether he was asleep or awake. This time the faces did not vanish. He blinked. The sheepskin had been taken

198

from the window and sunlight streamed over him.

"Gurgi? Kaw?" Taran murmured. "Fflewddur? What's happened to you? You look like half of yourself."

"You're hardly one to talk about appearances, old friend." The bard chuckled. "If you could see yourself, I'm sure you'd agree you look worse than I do."

Still baffled, Taran turned to Gurgi who had leaped up joyously and clapped his hands.

"Kindly master is well again!" Gurgi shouted. "He is well, without groanings and moanings, without shiverings and quiverings! And it is faithful, clever Gurgi who tends him!"

"That's true," agreed Fflewddur. "For the past two weeks he's fussed over you like a mother hen, and he couldn't have given you more care if you'd been one of his pet lambs!

"I rode straight as an arrow from Caer Dallben," the bard continued. "Ah—well—the truth of it is, I got lost for a time; then it began snowing. Llyan plowed through drifts up to her ears, and even she finally had to stop. For a while we sheltered in a cave—Great Belin, I thought I'd never see the light of day again." Fflewddur gestured at his tattered clothing. "It was the sort of journey that tends to make one rather unkempt. Not to mention three-fourths starved. Kaw was the one who happened to 199 find us, and he guided us along the clearer trails.

"As for Dallben," Fflewddur went on, "he was upset, considerably more than he wanted to show. Though all he said was 'Taran is not the herdsman's son, but whether or not he stays is a matter entirely of his own choosing.'

"And so I came back as fast as I could," the bard concluded. "Alas, I didn't reach you sooner." He shook his head. "Gurgi told me what happened."

"Craddoc longed for a son," Taran answered slowly, "as I longed for parentage. I wonder if I would not have been happier had I believed him. Though at the end, I think I did. Gurgi and I could have climbed to safety. For the sake of Craddoc, I sounded Eilonwy's horn. Had I done it sooner, perhaps he might have lived. He was a man of courage and good heart, a proud man. Now he is dead. I saved the signal to use in a worthy cause, and when I found one it was wasted."

"Wasted?" answered Fflewddur. "I think not. Since you did your best and didn't begrudge using it, I shouldn't call it wasted at all."

"There is more that you do not know," Taran said. He looked squarely at the bard. "My best? At first I thought to leave Craddoc on the ledge."

"Well, now," replied the bard, "each man has
his moment of fear. If we all behaved as we often

wished to there'd be sorry doings in Prydain. Count the deed, not the thought."

"In this I count my thought as much," Taran said in a cold voice. "It was not fear that held me back. Will you know the truth? I was ashamed to be base-born, so ashamed it sickened me. I would have left Craddoc to his death. Yes, left him to die!" he burst out. "Because I believed it would have set me free of him. I was ashamed to be the son of a herdsman. But no longer. Now my shame is for myself." He turned his face away and said no more.

The companions wintered in the cottage, and little by little Taran's strength came back. At the first thaw, when the valley sparkled with melting snow and the streams burst from their ice-bound courses, Taran stood silently in the dooryard and looked at the pale green summits, pondering what had long been in his heart.

"We'll soon be ready," said Fflewddur, who had come from seeing to Llyan and the steeds. "The passes should be clear. The Lake of Llunet can't be too far, and with Kaw to help us, we should reach it in no time."

"I've thought carefully on this," Taran replied. "All winter I've tried to decide what I should do, and never have I found an answer. But one thing is clear, and my mind is made up. I will not seek the Mirror."

"What's that you say?" cried Fflewddur. "Do I hear you aright? Give up your search? Now, of all times? After all you've gone through? Taran, my boy, you've regained your health, but not your wits!"

Taran shook his head. "I give it up. My quest has brought only grief to all of you. And for me, it's led me not to honor but to shame. Taran? Taran makes me sick at heart. I longed to be of noble birth, longed for it so much I believed it was true. A proud birthright was all that counted for me. Those who had none—even when I admired them, as I admired Aeddan, as I learned to admire Craddoc—I deemed them lesser because of it. Without knowing them, I judged them less than what they were. Now I see them as true men. Noble? They are far nobler than I.

"I am not proud of myself," Taran went on. "I may never be again. If I do find pride, I'll not find it in what I was or what I am, but what I may become. Not in my birth, but in myself."

"All things considered, then," replied the bard, "the best thing would be to pack our gear and start for Caer Dallben."

Taran shook his head. "I cannot face Dallben or Coll. One day, perhaps. Not now. I must make my own way, earn my own keep. Somehow, the robin must scratch for his own worms." He stopped sud-

denly and looked, wondering, at the bard. "Orddu—
those were her words. I heard them only with my
ears. Until now, I did not understand with my heart."

"Scratching for worms is unappetizing, to say
the best of it," Fflewddur answered. "But it's true,
everyone should have a skill. Take myself, for example. King though I am, as a bard you'll find none
better—" A harp string snapped, and for a moment it
appeared that several others might give way.

"Yes, well, aside from all that," Fflewddur
said hastily, "if you don't mean to go home, then I
suggest the Free Commots. The craftsmen there
might welcome a willing apprentice."

Taran thought for some moments, then
nodded. "So shall I do. Now will I scorn no man's
welcome."

The bard's face fell. "I—I fear I can't go with
you, old friend. There's my own realm waiting. True
enough, I'm happier wandering as a bard than sitting
as a king. But already I've been too long away."

"Then our ways must part again," Taran replied. "Will there ever be an end to saying farewell?"

"But Gurgi does not say farewell to kindly
master," cried Gurgi, as Fflewddur went to gather up
his gear. "No, no, humble Gurgi toils at his side!"

Taran bowed his head and turned away. "If
the day comes when I deserve your faithfulness that
will be prize enough for me."

"No, no!" protested Gurgi. "Not prizings! Gurgi only gives what is in his heart to give! He stays and asks nothing more. Once you comforted friendless Gurgi. Now let him comfort sorrowful master!"

Taran felt the creature's hand on his shoulder. "Dallben spoke truth, old friend," he murmured. "Staunchness and good sense? All that and more. But your comfort stands me in better stead than all the cleverness in Prydain."

Next morning Taran and Fflewddur took leave of one another for the second time. Despite the bard's protest that a Fflam could always find his way, Taran insisted on Kaw's going along as a guide. Once this task was done, Taran urged the crow to return to Caer Dallben or, if it pleased him better, to fly freely as he chose. "I'll not bind you to my journey," Taran said to Kaw, "for even I don't know where it may end."

"Then how do we fare?" cried Gurgi. "Faithful Gurgi follows, oh, yes! But where does kindly master begin?"

The valley seemed suddenly empty as Taran stood, unanswering, looking at the silent cottage and the small mound of stones marking Craddoc's resting place. "Times there were," Taran said, almost to himself, "when I believed I was building my own prison with my own hands. Now I wonder if I shall ever labor as well and gain as much."

He turned to the waiting Gurgi. "Where?" He knelt, plucked a handful of dry grass from the turf, and cast it into the air. The freshening wind bore the blades eastward, toward the Free Commots.

"There," Taran said. "As the wind blows, so do we follow it."

Since neither Taran nor Gurgi wished to leave the sheep behind, the wayfarers departed from the valley with the small flock bleating after them. Taran intended offering the animals to the first farmstead with good grazing land, yet several days passed and he saw no inhabited place. The two companions had started in a southeasterly direction, but Taran soon gave Melynlas free rein and, though aware the stallion was bearing more east than south, he paid little heed until they drew near the banks of a wide, rapid-flowing river.

Here, the pasture stretched broad and fair. Ahead he glimpsed an empty sheepfold; he noticed no flock, but the gate of the enclosure stood open as though awaiting the animals' return at any moment. The low-roofed cottage and sheds were neat and well-kept. A pair of shaggy goats browsed near the door-yard. Taran blinked in surprise, for set about the cottage were all manner of woven baskets, some large, some small, some rising on stilts, and others seemingly dropped at random. Several trees by the river held wooden platforms, and along the riverbank itself Taran caught sight of what appeared to be a weir of carefully woven branches. Wooden stakes secured a number of nets and fishing lines drifting in the current.

Puzzling over this farmhold, surely the strangest he had seen, Taran drew closer, dismounted, and as he did so a tall figure ambled from the shed and made his way toward the companions. Taran glimpsed the farm wife peering from the cottage window. At the same time, as if out of nowhere, half-a-dozen children of different ages burst into sight and began running and skipping toward the flock, laughing gaily and shouting to one another: "They're here! They're here!" Seeing Gurgi, they turned their attention from the sheep to cluster around him, clapping their hands in delight and calling out such merry-hearted greetings that the astonished creature could only laugh and clap his own hands in return.

The man who stood before Taran was thin as a stick with lank hair tumbling over his brow and blue eyes bright as a bird's. Indeed, his narrow shoulders and spindly legs made him look like a crane or stork. His jacket was too short in the arms, too long in the body, and his garments seemed pieced together with patches of all sizes, shapes, and colors.

"I am Llonio Son of Llonwen," he said, with a friendly grin and a wave of his hand. "A good greeting to you, whoever you may be."

Taran bowed courteously. "My name—my name is Taran."

"No more than that?" said Llonio. "As a name, my friend, it's cropped a little short." He laughed good-naturedly. "Shall I call you Taran Son of Nobody? Taran of Nowhere? Since you're alive and breathing, obviously you're the son of two parents. And you've surely ridden here from somewhere else."

"Call me, then, a wanderer," Taran replied.

"Taran Wanderer? So be it, if that suits you." Llonio's glance was curious, but he asked no further.

When Taran then spoke of seeking pasture for the sheep, Llonio nodded briskly.

"Why, here shall they stay, and my thanks to you," he exclaimed. "There's no grazing fresher and sweeter, and no sheepfold safer. We've seen to that and labored since the first thaw to make it so."

"But I fear they may crowd your own flock," Taran said, though he admired Llonio's pastureland and the stoutly built enclosure, and would have been well content to leave the sheep with him.

"My flock?" Llonio answered, laughing. "I 207

had none until this moment! Though we've been hoping and waiting and the children have been talking of little else. A lucky wind it was that brought you to us. Goewin, my wife, needs wool to clothe our young ones. Now we'll have fleece and to spare."

"Wait, wait," put in Taran, altogether baffled, "do you mean you cleared a pasture and built a sheepfold without having any sheep at all? I don't understand. That was work in vain—"

"Was it now?" asked Llonio, winking shrewdly. "If I hadn't, would you be offering me a fine flock in the first place; and in the second, would I have the place to keep them? Is that not so?"

"But you couldn't have known," Taran began.

"Ah, ah," Llonio chuckled, "why, look you, I knew that with any kind of luck a flock of sheep was bound to come along one day. Everything else does! Now honor us by stopping here a while. Our fare can't match our thanks, but we'll feast you as best we can."

Before Taran could answer, Llonio bent down to one of the little girls who was staring round-eyed at Gurgi. "Now then, Gwenlliant, run see if the brown hen's chosen to lay us an egg today." He turned to Taran. "The brown hen's a moody creature," he said. "But when she has a mind to, she puts down a handsome egg." He then set the rest of the children running off on different tasks, while Taran and Gurgi watched astonished at the hustle and bustle in this most peculiar household. Llonio led the two into the cottage where Goewin gave them a warm welcome and bade them sit by the hearth. In no time Gwenlliant was back holding an egg in outstretched hands.

"An egg!" cried Llonio, taking it from her, raising it aloft, and peering as if he had never seen one before. "An egg it is! The finest the brown hen's given us! Look at the size! The shape! Smooth as glass and not a crack on it. We'll feast well on this, my friends."

At first Taran saw nothing extraordinary in the egg which Llonio praised so highly; but, caught up by the man's good spirits, Taran to his own surprise found himself looking at the egg as though he, too, had never seen one. In Llonio's hands the shell seemed to sparkle so brightly, to curve so gracefully and beautifully that even Gurgi marveled at it, and Taran watched almost with regret as Goewin cracked such a precious egg into a large earthen bowl. Nevertheless, if Llonio intended sharing it among his numerous family, Taran told himself, the fare would indeed be meager.

Yet, as Goewin stirred the contents of the bowl, the children crowded one after the other into the cottage, all bearing something that made Llonio call out cheerily at each discovery.

"Savory herbs!" he cried. "That's splendid! Chop them up well. And here—what's this, a handful of flour? Better and better! We'll need that pot of milk the goat's given us, too. A bit of cheese? Just the thing!" Then he clapped his hands delightedly as the last and smallest child held up a fragment of honeycomb. "What luck! The bees have left us honey from their winter store."

Goewin, meanwhile, was busy popping all these finds into the bowl and, before Taran's eyes, the contents soon filled it nearly to the brim. Even then, his surprise did not end. Goewin deftly poured the mixture onto a sheet of metal which, Taran was quite certain, was nothing else but a warrior's shield hammered flat, and held it over the glowing embers. Within moments, the scent of cooking filled the cottage, Gurgi's mouth watered, and in no time the farm wife drew a dappled golden cake nearly as big as a cartwheel from the fireplace.

Llonio quickly sliced it into pieces and to Taran's amazement there was not only enough for all but some left over. He ate his fill of the most delicious egg he ever tasted—if egg it could now be called— and not even Gurgi could eat more.

"Now then," said Llonio, when they had finished, "I'll see to my nets. Come along, if you like."

CHAPTER XVII

The Weir

hile Gurgi lingered in the cottage, Taran followed Llonio to the riverbank. On the way, whistling merrily through his teeth, Llonio stopped to peer into the baskets, and Taran noticed one of them held a large bee hive undoubtedly the source of the honey which had sweetened Goewin's cake. The rest, however, stood empty. Llonio merely shrugged his shoulders.

"No matter," he said. "Something will surely fill them later. Last time a flock of wild geese flew down to rest. You should have seen the feathers left after they'd gone. Enough to stuff cushions for every one of us!"

By now they reached the river, which Llonio named as Small Avren since, farther south, it flowed into Great Avren itself. "Small it is," he said, "but sooner or later whatever you might wish comes floating along." As if to prove his words he began hauling vigorously at the net staked along the bank. It came up empty, as did the fishing lines. Undismayed, Llonio shrugged again. "Tomorrow, very likely."

"How then," Taran exclaimed, feeling perplexed as he had ever been, "do you count on baskets and nets to bring you what you need?" He looked at the man in astonishment.

"That I do," replied Llonio, laughing good-naturedly. "My holding is small; I work it as best as I can. For the rest—why, look you, if I know one thing, it's this: Life's a matter of luck. Trust it, and a man's bound to find what he seeks, one day or the next."

"Perhaps so," Taran admitted, "but what if it takes longer than that? Or never comes at all?"

"Be that as it may," answered Llonio, grinning. "If I fret over tomorrow, I'll have little joy today."

So saying, he clambered nimbly onto the weir, which Taran now saw was made not to bar the flow of water but to strain and sift the current. Balancing atop this odd construction, seeming more cranelike than ever as he bobbed up and down, bending to poke and pry among the osiers, Llonio soon gave a glad cry and waved excitedly.

Taran hurriedly picked his way across the dam to join him. His face fell, however, when he reached Llonio's side. What had caused the man's joyful shout was no more than a discarded horse bridle.

"Alas," said Taran, disappointed, "there's little

use in that. The bit's missing and the rein's worn through."

"So be it, so be it," replied Llonio. "That's what Small Avren's brought us today, and it will serve, one way or another." He slung the dripping bridle over his shoulder, scrambled from the dam, and with Taran following him set off with long strides through the grove of trees fringing the river.

In a while Llonio, whose sharp eyes darted everywhere at once, cried out again and stooped at the bottom of a gnarled elm. Amid the roots and for some distance around, mushrooms sprouted abundantly.

"Pluck them up, Wanderer," Llonio exclaimed. "There's our supper for tonight. The finest mushrooms I've seen! Tender and tasty! We're in luck today!" Quickly gathering his finds, Llonio popped them into a sack dangling from his belt and set off again.

Following Llonio's rambling, halting now and then to cull certain herbs or roots, the day sped so swiftly it was nearly over before Taran realized it had begun. Llonio's sack being full, the two turned their steps back to the cottage, taking a path different from the way they had come. As they ambled along, Taran caught his foot on a jutting edge of stone and he tumbled head over heels.

"Your luck is better than mine," Taran

laughed ruefully. "You've found your mushrooms, and I, no more than a pair of bruised shins!"

"Not so, not so!" protested Llonio, hastily scraping away the loam partly covering the stone. Look you, now! Have you ever seen one so shaped? Round as a wheel and smooth as an egg. A windfall it is that needs only the picking up!"

If a windfall, Taran thought, it was the hardest and heaviest he had stumbled on, for Llonio now insisted on unearthing the flat rock. They did so with much digging and heaving and, carrying it between them struggled back to the farmhold, where Llonio rolled it into the shed already bursting with an odd array of churn handles, strips of cloth, horse trappings, thongs, hanks of cord, and all the harvest of his weir, nets, and baskets.

Over the cookfire, the mushrooms, eked out with the leftover griddle cake and a handful of early vegetables the children had found, simmered so deliciously that Taran and Gurgi needed no urging to stay for the repast. As night fell Taran welcomed the family's invitation to rest by the hearth. Gurgi, stuffed and contented, began snoring instantly. And Taran, for the first time in many days, slept soundly and dreamlessly.

The next morning was bright and crisp. Taran woke to find the sun high, and though he had meant to saddle Melynlas and be on his way he did not do so. If Llonio's weir had yielded little the day before, the night current had more than made up for it. A great sack of wheat had somehow become tangled with a cluster of dead branches which served as a raft and thus had floated downstream undampened by the river. Goewin, without delay, brought out a large stone quern to grind the grain into meal. All took a hand in the task, the children from eldest to youngest, even Llonio himself; Taran did his share willingly, though he found the quern heavy and cumbersome, as did Gurgi.

"Oh tiresome millings," Gurgi cried. "Gurgi's poor fingers are filled with achings, and his arms with strainings and painings!"

Nevertheless, he finished his turn; although by the time enough meal had been ground, another day had nearly sped by, and once more Llonio urged the wayfarers to share his hospitality. Taran did not refuse. Indeed, as he stretched by the fire, he admitted to himself he had secretly hoped Llonio would suggest it.

During the next few days, Taran's heart was easier than it had been since he chose to abandon his quest. The children, shy with him at first as he with them, had become his fast friends, and frolicked with him as much as they did with Gurgi. With Llonio, each day he visited the nets, the baskets, and the weir, sometimes returning empty-handed and sometimes laden with whatever strange assortment the wind or current brought. In the beginning he had seen no value in these odds and ends, but Llonio found a use for nearly all. A cartwheel was turned into a spinning wheel, parts of the horse-bridle made belts for the children, a saddlebag became a pair of boots; and Taran shortly realized there was little the family needed that did not, late or soon, appear from nowhere; and there was nothing—an egg, a mushroom, a handful of feathers delicate as ferns—that was not held to be a treasure.

"In a way," Taran told Gurgi, "Llonio's richer than Lord Gast is or ever will be. Not only that, he's the luckiest man in Prydain! I envy no man's riches," Taran added. Then he sighed and shook his head. "But I wish I had Llonio's luck."

When he repeated this to Llonio, the man only grinned and winked at him. "Luck, Wanderer? One day, if you're lucky, I'll tell you the secret of it." Beyond that, Llonio would say no more.

At this time a thought had begun taking shape in Taran's mind. Nearly all of Llonio's finds had been put to one use or another—save the flat stone which still lay in the shed. "But I wonder," he told Llonio, "I wonder if it couldn't serve to grind meal better than the quern . . ."

"How then?" cried Llonio, greatly pleased. "If you think it can, do as you see fit."

Still pondering his idea, Taran roamed the woods until he came upon another stone of much the same size as the first. "That's a stroke of luck,"he laughed, as Llonio helped him drag it back.

Llonio grinned. "So it is, so it is."

During the several days following, Taran, with Gurgi's eager help, toiled unceasingly. In a corner of the shed he set one stone firmly in the ground and the other above it. In this, he laboriously hollowed out a hole and, using the leftover harness leathers, in it he affixed a long pole that reached up through an opening in the roof. At the top of the pole he attached frames of wood, over which he stretched large squares of cloth.

"But this is no quern," Gurgi cried when at last it was done. "It is a ship for boatings and floatings! But there is no ship, only mast with sails!"

"We shall see," Taran answered, calling Llonio to judge his handiwork.

For a moment the family stood puzzled at Taran's peculiar structure. Then, as the wind stirred, the roughly fashioned sails caught the current of the breeze. The mastlike pole shuddered and creaked, and for a breathless instant Taran feared all his work would come tumbling about his ears. But it held fast, the sails bellied out and began turning, slowly at first, then faster and faster, while below, in the shed, the upper stone whirled merrily. Goewin hastened to 217 throw grain into Taran's makeshift mill. In no time, out poured meal finer than any the quern had ground. The children clapped their hands and shouted gleefully; Gurgi yelped in astonishment; and Llonio laughed until the tears ran down his cheeks.

"Wanderer," he cried, "you've made much from little, and done it better than ever I could!"

Over the next few days the mill not only ground the family's grain, Taran also struck on a means of using it as a sharpening stone for Llonio's tools. Looking at his handiwork, Taran felt a stirring of pride for the first time since leaving Craddoc's valley. But with it came a vague restiveness.

"By rights," he told Gurgi, "I should be more than happy to dwell here all my life. I've found peace and friendship—and a kind of hope, as well. It's eased my heart like balm on a wound." He hesitated. "Yet, somehow Llonio's way is not mine. A spur drives me to seek more than what Small Avren brings. What I seek, I do not know. But, alas, I know it is not here."

He spoke then with Llonio and regretfully told him he must take up his journeying again. This time, sensing Taran's decision firmly made, Llonio did not urge him to stay, and they bade each other farewell.

"And yet," Taran said, as he swung astride

Melynlas, "alas, you never told me the secret of your luck."

"Secret?" replied Llonio. "Have you not already guessed? Why, my luck's no greater than yours or any man's. You need only sharpen your eyes to see your luck when it comes, and sharpen your wits to use what falls into your hands."

Taran gave Melynlas rein, and with Gurgi at his side rode slowly from the banks of Small Avren. As he turned to wave a last farewell, he heard Llonio calling after him, "Trust your luck, Taran Wanderer. But don't forget to put out your nets!"

CHAPTER XVIII

The Free Commots

From Small Avren they wended eastward at an easy pace, halting as it pleased them, sleeping on the turf or sheltering at one of the many farmsteads among the rich green vales. This was the land of the Free Commots, of cottages clustering in loose circles, rimmed by cultivated fields and pastures. Taran found the Commot folk courteous and hospitable. Though he named himself only as Taran Wanderer, the dwellers in these hamlets and villages respected his privacy and asked nothing of his birthplace, rank, or destination.

Taran and Gurgi had ridden into the outskirts of Commot Cenarth when Taran reined up Melynlas at a long, low-roofed shed from which rang the sound of hammer on anvil. Within, he found the smith, a barrel-chested, leather-aproned man with a stubbly black beard and a great shock of black hair bristly as a brush. His eyelashes were scorched, grime and soot smudged his face; sparks rained on his bare shoulders but he seemed to count them no more than fireflies. In a voice like stones rattling on a bronze shield he roared out a song in time with his hammer strokes so loudly that Taran judged the man's lungs as leathery as his bellows. While Gurgi cautiously drew back from the shower of sparks, Taran called a greeting, scarcely able to make himself heard above the din.

"Master Smith," he said, bowing deeply as the man at last caught sight of him and put down the hammer, "I am called Taran Wanderer and journey seeking a craft to help me earn my bread. I know a little of your art and ask you to teach me more. I have no gold or silver to pay you, but name any task and I will do it gladly."

"Away with you!" shouted the smith. "Tasks I have aplenty, but no time for teaching others to do them."

"Is time what lacks?" Taran said, glancing shrewdly at the smith. "I've heard it said that a man must be a true master of his craft if he would teach it."

"Hold!" roared the smith as Taran was about to turn away, and he snatched up the hammer as if he meant to throw it at Taran's head. "You doubt my skill? I've flattened men on my anvil for less! Skill? In all the Free Commots none has greater than Hevydd Son of Hirwas!"

With that he seized the tongs, drew a bar of red-hot iron from the roaring furnace, flung it on the 221 anvil, and set to hammering with such quick strokes that Taran could hardly follow the movement of Hevydd's muscular arm; and suddenly there formed at the end of the bar a hawthorn blossom perfect in every turn of leaf and petal.

Taran looked at it in astonishment and admiration. "Never have I seen work so deftly done."

"Nor will you see it elsewhere," Hevydd answered, at pains to hide a proud grin. "But what tale do you tell me? You know the shaping of metal? The secrets are not given to many. Even I have not gained them all." Angrily he shook his bristly head. "The deepest? They lie hidden in Annuvin, stolen by Arawn Death-Lord. Lost they are. Lost forever to Prydain.

"But here, take these," ordered the smith, pressing the tongs and hammer into Taran's hands. "Beat the bar smooth as it was, and quickly, before it cools. Show me what strength you have in those chicken wings of yours."

Taran strode to the anvil and, as Coll had taught him long ago, did his best to straighten the rapidly cooling iron. The smith, folding his huge arms, eyed him critically for a time, then burst into loud laughter.

"Enough, enough!" cried Hevydd. "You speak truth. Of the art, indeed, you know little. And yet," he added, rubbing his chin with a battered thumb nearly as thick as a fist, "and yet, you have the sense of it." He looked closely at Taran. "But have you courage to stand up to fire? To fight hot iron with only hammer and tongs?"

"Teach me the craft," Taran replied. "You'll have no need to teach me courage."

"Boldly said!" cried Hevydd, clapping Taran on the shoulder. "I'll temper you well in my forge! Prove yourself to me and I'll vow to make a smith of you. Now, to begin . . ." His eye fell on Taran's empty scabbard. "Once, it would seem, you bore a blade."

"Once I did," Taran answered. "But it is long gone, and now I journey weaponless."

"Then you shall make a sword," commanded Hevydd. "And when you've done, you'll tell me which is harder labor: smiting or smithing!"

To this Taran learned the answer soon enough. The next several days were the most toil-some he had ever spent. He thought, at first, the smith would set him to work shaping one of the many bars already in the forge. But Hevydd had no such intention.

"What, start when half the work is done?" Hevydd snorted. "No, no, my lad. You'll forge a sword from beginning to end."

Thus, the first task Hevydd gave Taran was gathering fuel for the furnace, and from dawn to dusk Taran stoked the fire until he saw the forge as a roaring, flame-tongued monster that could never eat its fill. Even then the work had only begun, for Hevydd soon put him to shoveling in a very mountain of stones, then smelting out the metal they bore. By the time the bar itself was cast, Taran's face and arms were scorched and blackened, and his hands were covered with more blisters than skin. His back ached; his ears rang with all the clank and clatter and with Hevydd's voice shouting orders and instructions. Gurgi, who had offered to pump the bellows, never faltered even when a cloud of sparks burst and flew into his shaggy hair, singeing it away in patches until he looked as if a flock of birds had plucked him to make their nests.

"Life's a forge!" cried the smith, as Taran, his brow streaming, beat at the strip of metal. "Yes, and hammer and anvil, too! You'll be roasted, smelted, and pounded, and you'll scarce know what's happening to you. But stand boldly to it! Metal's worthless till it's shaped and tempered!"

Despite the weariness that made him drop gratefully at day's end to the straw pallet in the shed, Taran's heart quickened and his spirits rose as the blade little by little took shape on the anvil. The heavy hammer seemed to weigh more each time he lifted it; but at last, with a joyous cry, he flung it down and raised the finished sword, well-wrought and balanced, gleaming brightly in the light of the forge.

"A handsome weapon, master smith!" he cried. "As fair as the one I bore!"

"What, then?" Hevydd exclaimed. "Have you done your work so well? Would you trust your life to a blade untried?" He flung out a burly arm toward a wooden block in a corner of the forge. "Strike hard," he commanded. "The flat, the edge, and the point."

Proudly Taran raised the sword high and swung it down to the block. The weapon shuddered with the force of the blow, a sharp crack and clang smote his ears as the blade shattered and the shards went flying in all directions.

Taran shouted in dismay and could have wept as he stared, disbelieving, at the broken hilt still clutched in his hand. He turned and gave Hevydd a despairing glance.

"So ho!" cried the smith, not at all distressed by Taran's wretched and rueful expression. "Did you think to gain a worthy blade at first go?" He laughed loudly and shook his head.

"Then what must I do?" Taran cried, appalled at Hevydd's words.

"Do?" the smith retorted. "What else but start anew?"

And so they did, but this time for Taran there remained little of his joyous hopes. He labored grimly and doggedly, all the more dejected when Hevydd ordered him to cast aside two new blades even before they were tempered, judging them already flawed. The reek of hot metal clung in his nostrils and flavored even the food he hastily swallowed; the billows of steam from the great quenching tub choked him as if he were breathing clouds of scalding fog; the ceaseless din almost addled his wits; until indeed he felt it was himself, not the blade, being hammered.

The next blade he shaped seemed to him ugly, dinted, and scarred, without the fair proportions of the first, and this too he would have cast aside had not the smith ordered him to finish it.

"This may well serve," Hevydd told him confidently, despite the doubtful look Taran gave him.

Again Taran strode to the block and raised the sword. Doing his best to shatter the ungraceful weapon, he brought it down with all his strength. The blade rang like a bell. This time it was the block that split in two.

"Now," said Hevydd quietly. "That's a blade worth bearing."

Then he clapped his hands and seized Taran's arm. "You've strength in those chicken wings after all! You've proved yourself as well as you proved the blade. Stay, lad, and I'll teach you all I know."

Taran said nothing for a time, but looked, not without pride, at the new-forged blade. "You have already taught me much," he said at last to Hevydd, "though I lost what I had hoped to gain. For I had hoped I was indeed a swordsmith. I have learned that I am not."

"How then!" cried Hevydd. "You've the makings of an honest swordsmith, as good as any in Prydain."

"It cheers me to think that may be true," Taran answered. "But I know in my heart your craft is not mine. A spur drove me from Small Avren, and it drives me now. And so must I journey, even if I wished to stay."

The smith nodded. "You are well-named, Wanderer. So be it. I ask no man to go against his heart. Keep the blade in token of friendship. Yours it is, more so than any other, for you forged it with your own hands."

"It's not a noble weapon, and thus it suits me all the more," Taran laughed, glancing at the ungainly sword. "Lucky it was that I didn't have to make a dozen before it."

"Luck?" snorted Hevydd, as Taran and Gurgi took leave of him. "Not so! More labor than luck.

Life's a forge, say I! Face the pounding; don't fear the proving; and you'll stand well against any hammer and anvil!"

With Hevydd the Smith waving a sooty hand in farewell, the companions traveled on, bearing northward along the rich valley of Great Avren. A few days of easy riding through pleasant countryside brought them to the edge of Commot Gwenith. Here, a shower suddenly began pelting down on them, and the wayfarers galloped for the first shelter they could find.

It was a cluster of sheds, stables, chicken roosts, and storehouses seeming to ramble in all directions, but as Taran dismounted and hastened to the cottage amid the maze of buildings, he realized all were linked by covered walkways or flagstoned paths, and whichever he followed would sooner or later have brought him to the doorway that opened almost before he knocked on it.

"Come in, and a good greeting to you!" called a voice crackling like twigs in a fire.

As Gurgi scuttled inside to escape the teeming rain, Taran saw a bent old woman cloaked in gray beckoning him to the hearth. Her long hair was white as the wool on the distaff hanging from her belt of plaited cords. Below her short-girt robe, her bony shins looked thin and hard as spindles. A web of wrinkles covered her face; her cheeks were withered; but for all her years she gave no sign of frailty, as though time had only toughened and seasoned her; and her gray eyes were sharp and bright as a pair of new needles.

"I am Dwyvach Weaver-Woman," she replied, as Taran bowed courteously and told her his name. "Taran Wanderer?" she repeated with a tart smile. "From the look of you, I'd say you've indeed been wandering. More than you've been washing. And that's clear as the warp and weft on my loom."

"Yes, yes!" cried Gurgi. "See loom of weavings! See windings and bindings! So many it makes Gurgi's poor tender head swim with twirlings and whirlings!"

Taran for the first time noticed a high loom standing like a giant harp of a thousand strings in a corner of the cottage. Around it were stacked bobbins of thread of all colors; from the rafters dangled skeins of yarn, hanks of wool and flax; on the walls hung lengths of finished fabrics, some of bright hue and simple design, others of subtler craftsmanship and patterns more difficult to follow. Taran gazed astonished at the endless variety, then turned to the weaver-woman of Gwenith.

"This calls for skill beyond anything I know," he said admiringly. "How is such work done?"

"How done?" The weaver-woman chuckled. "It would take me more breath to tell than you have ears to listen. But if you look, you shall see."

So saying, she hobbled to the loom, climbed to the bench in front of it, and with surprising vigor began plying the shuttle back and forth, all the while working her feet on the treadles below, hardly pausing to glance at her handiwork. At last she stopped, cocked her head at Taran, fixed him with her sharp gray eyes, and said, "Thus is it done, Wanderer, as all things are, each in its own way, thread by thread."

Taran's amazement had grown all the more. "This would I gladly learn," he said eagerly. "The craft of the swordsmith was not mine. Perhaps the craft of the weaver may be. I pray you, will you teach it to me?"

"That I will, since you ask," replied Dwyvach. "But mind you: It is one thing to admire a well-woven bit of cloth and another to sit yourself before the loom."

"My thanks to you," Taran exclaimed. "I'll not fear to labor at your loom. With Hevydd the Smith, I didn't shrink from hot iron or the flames of his forge, and a weaver's shuttle is a lighter burden than a smith's hammer."

"Think you so?" Dwyvach asked, with a dry chuckle that sounded like knitting needles clicking together. "Then what shall you weave to begin with?'' she went on, eyeing him sharply. "Taran Wanderer you call yourself? Taran Threadbare would be more like it! Would you weave yourself a new cloak? Thus you'll gain something to put on your back, and I'll see what skill you have in your fingers."

Taran willingly agreed; but next day, instead of teaching him weaving, Dwyvach led the companions to one of her many chambers, which Taran saw full nearly to bursting with piles of wool.

"Tease out the thorns, pick out the cockleburs," the weaver-woman ordered. "Comb it, card it—carefully, Wanderer, or when your cloak is done you'll feel it's made of thistles instead of wool!"

The size of the task ahead of him made Taran despair of ever finishing, but he and Gurgi started the painstaking work, with Dwyvach herself lending a hand. The aged weaver-woman, Taran soon learned, had not only a tart tongue but a keen eye. Nothing escaped her; she spied the smallest knot, speck, or flaw, and brought Taran's attention to it with a sharp rap from her distaff to his knuckles. But what smarted Taran more than the distaff was to learn that Dwyvach, despite her years, could work faster, longer, and harder than he himself. At the end of each day Taran's eyes were bleary, his fingers raw, and his head nodded wearily; yet the old weaver-woman was bright and spry as if the day had scarce begun.

Nevertheless, the work at last was finished. But now Dwyvach set him in front of a huge spinning wheel. "The finest wool is useless until it's spun to thread," the weaver woman told him. "So you'd best begin learning that, as well."

"But spinnings are woman's toilings!" Gurgi protested. "No, no, spinnings are not fitting for bold and clever weaver-men!"

"Indeed!" snorted Dwyvach. "Then sit you down and learn otherwise. I've heard men complain of doing woman's work, and women complain of doing man's work," she added, fastening her bony thumb and forefinger on Gurgi's ear and marching him to a stool beside Taran, "but I've never heard the *work* complain of who did it, so long as it got done!"

And so, under Dwyvach's watchful eye, Taran and Gurgi spun thread and filled bobbins during the next few days. Chastened by Dwyvach's words, Gurgi did his best to help, though all too often the hapless creature managed only to tangle himself in the long strands. Next, Dwyvach took the companions to a shed where pots of dye bubbled over a fire. Here, Taran fared no better than Gurgi, for when the yarn was at last dyed, he was bespattered from head to toe with colors, and Gurgi himself looked like a rainbow suddenly sprouting hair.

Not until all these other tasks were done to

Dwyvach's satisfaction did she take Taran to a weaving room; and there his heart sank, for the loom stood bare and stark as a leafless tree.

"How then?" clucked the weaver-woman as Taran gave her a rueful glance. "The loom must be threaded. Did I not tell you: All things are done step by step and strand by strand?"

"Hevydd the Smith told me life was a forge," Taran sighed, as he laboriously tried to reckon the countless threads needed, "and I think I'll be well-tempered before my cloak is finished."

"Life a forge?" said the weaver-woman. "A loom, rather, where lives and days intertwine; and wise he is who can learn to see the pattern. But if you mean to have a new cloak, you'd do better to work more and chatter less. Or did you hope for a host of spiders to come and labor for you?"

Even after deciding on the pattern, and threading the loom, Taran still saw only a hopeless, confusing tangle of threads. The cloth was painfully slow in forming and at the end of a long day he had little more than a hand's breadth of fabric to show for all his toil.

"Did I ever think a weaver's shuttle a light burden?" Taran sighed. "It feels heavier than hammer, tongs, and anvil all together!"

"It's not the shuttle that burdens you," answered Dwyvach, "but lack of skill, a heavy burden, Wanderer, that only one thing can lift."

"What secret is that?" Taran cried. "Teach it to me now or my cloak will never be done."

But Dwyvach only smiled. "It is patience, Wanderer. As for teaching it, that I cannot do. It is both the first thing and the last thing you must learn for yourself."

Taran gloomily went back to work, sure he would be as ancient as Dwyvach before finishing the garment. Nevertheless, as his hands became used to the task the shuttle darted back and forth like a fish among reeds, and the cloth grew steadily on the loom; though Dwyvach was satisfied with his progress, Taran, to his own surprise, was not.

"The pattern," he murmured, frowning. "It— I don't know, somehow it doesn't please me."

"Now then, Wanderer," replied Dwyvach, "no man put a sword to your throat; the choice of pattern was your own."

"That it was," Taran admitted. "But now I see it closely, I would rather have chosen another."

"Ah, ah," said Dwyvach, with her dry chuckle, "in that case you have but one of two things to do. Either finish a cloak you'll be ill-content to wear, or unravel it and start anew. For the loom weaves only the pattern set upon it."

Taran stared a long while at his handiwork. At last he took a deep breath, sighed, and shook his head. "So be it. I'll start anew."

Over the next few days he ruefully un-threaded and rethreaded the loom. But after it was ready and he began weaving once again, he was delighted to find the cloth grow faster than ever it had done before, and his spirits rose with his new-found skill. When the cloak at last was done, he held it up proudly.

"This is far better than what I had," he cried. "But I doubt I'll ever be able to wear a cloak again without thinking of every thread!"

Gurgi shouted triumphantly and Dwyvach bobbed her head in approval.

"Well-woven," she said. Her expression had lost much of its tartness and she looked fondly at Taran, seeming to smile within herself. "You have skill in your fingers, Wanderer," she said, with unaccustomed gentleness. "Enough to make you one of the finest weavers in Prydain. And if my distaff and your knuckles met more often than you liked, it was because I deemed you worth reproving. Dwell in my house, if you choose, work at my loom, and what I know I will teach you."

Taran did not answer immediately, and as he hesitated, the weaver-woman smiled and spoke again.

"I know what is in your heart, Wanderer," she said. "A young man's way is restless; yes, and a young girl's too—I'm not so gone in years that I've forgotten. Your face tells me it is not your wish to stay in Commot Gwenith."

Taran nodded. "As much as I hoped to be a swordsmith, so I hoped to be a weaver. But you speak truth. This is not the way I would follow."

"Then must we say farewell," answered the weaver-woman. "But mind you," she added, in her usual sharp tone, "if life is a loom, the pattern you weave is not so easily unraveled."

Taran and Gurgi set off again, still journeying northward, and soon Commot Gwenith was far behind them. Though Taran wore his new cloak on his shoulders and his new blade at his side, his pleasure in them shortly gave way to disquiet. The words of Dwyvach lingered in his mind, and his thoughts turned to another loom in the distant Marshes of Morva.

"And what of Orddu?" he said. "Does she weave with more than threads? The robin has truly been scratching for his worms. But have I indeed chosen my own pattern, or am I no more than a thread on her loom? If that be so, then I fear it's a thread serving little purpose. At any rate," he added, with a rueful laugh, "it's a long and tangled one."

But these gloomy thoughts flew from his mind when, some days later, Melynlas bore him to the top of a rise and he looked down on the fairest Commot he had ever seen. A tall stand of firs and hemlocks circled broad, well-tended fields, green and abundant. White, thatch-roofed cottages sparkled in shafts of sunlight. The air itself seemed different to him, cool and touched with the sharp scent of evergreens. His heart quickened as he watched, and a strange excitement filled him.

Gurgi had ridden up beside him. "Kindly master, can we not stop here?"

"Yes," Taran murmured, his eyes never leaving the fields and cottages. "Yes. Here shall we rest."

He urged Melynlas down the slope, with Gurgi cantering eagerly behind him. Crossing a shallow stream, Taran reined up at the sight of a hale old man digging busily near the water's edge. Beside him stood a pair of wooden buckets on a yoke, and into these he carefully poured spadefuls of pale brown earth. His iron-gray hair and beard were cropped short; despite his age, his arms seemed as brawny as those of Hevydd the Smith.

"A good greeting to you, master delver," Taran called. "What place is this?"

The man turned, wiped his deeply lined brow with a forearm, and looked at Taran with keen blue eyes. "The water your horse is standing in—and churning to mud, by the way—is Fernbrake Stream. The Commot? This is Commot Merin."

CHAPTER XIX

The Potter's Wheel

"'ve told you where you are," the man went on good-naturedly, as Taran dismounted at the bank of the stream. "Now might you be willing to tell me who you are, and what brings you to a place whose name you must ask? Have you lost your way and found Merin when you sought another Commot?"

"I am called Wanderer," Taran replied. "As for losing my way," he added with a laugh, "I can't say that I have, for I'm not sure myself where my path lies."

"Then Merin is as fair a place as any to break your journey," the man said. "Come along, if you'd see what hospitality I can offer the two of you."

As the man dropped a last spadeful of clay into the wooden buckets, Taran stepped forward and offered to carry them; and, since the man did not refuse, set his shoulders under the yoke. But the buckets were heavier than Taran reckoned. His brow soon burst out in sweat; he could barely stagger along under the load he felt doubling at every pace;

and the hut to which the man pointed seemed to grow farther instead of closer.

"If you seek daub to mend your chimney," Taran gasped, "you've come a long way to find it!"

"You've not caught the trick of that yoke," said the man, grinning broadly at Taran's effort. He shouldered the buckets, which Taran gladly gave back, and strode along so briskly, despite the weight of his burden, that he nearly outdistanced the companions. Arriving at a long shed, he poured the clay into a great wooden vat, then beckoned the wayfarers to enter his hut.

Inside Taran saw racks and shelves holding earthenware of all kinds, vessels of plain baked clay, graceful jars, and among these, at random, pieces whose craftsmanship and beauty made him catch his breath. Only once, in the treasure house of Lord Gast, had he set eyes on handiwork such as this. He turned, astonished, to the old man who had begun laying dishes and bowls on an oaken table.

"When I asked if you sought daub to mend your chimney I spoke foolishly," Taran said, humbly bowing. "If this is your work, I have seen some of it before, and I know you: Annlaw Clay-Shaper."

The potter nodded. "My work it is. If you've seen it, it may be that indeed you do know me. For I am old at my craft, Wanderer, and no longer sure 239 where the clay ends and Annlaw begins—or, in truth, if they're not one and the same."

Taran looked closer at the vessels crowding the hut, at the newly finished wine bowl shaped even more skillfully than the one in Lord Gast's trove, at the long, clay-spattered tables covered with jars of paints, pigments, and glazes. Now he saw in wonder that what he had first taken for common scullery-ware was as beautiful, in its own way, as the wine bowl. All had come from a master's hand. He turned to Annlaw.

"It was told me," Taran said, "that one piece of your making is worth more than all of a cantrev lord's treasure house, and I well believe it. And here," he shook his head in amazement, "this is a treasure house in itself."

"Yes, yes!" Gurgi cried. "Oh, skillful potter gains riches and fortunes from clever shapings!"

"Riches and fortune?" replied Annlaw smiling. "Food for my table, rather. Most of these pots and bowls I send to the small Commots where the folk have no potter of their own. As I give what they need, they give what I need; and treasure is what I need the least. My joy is in the craft, not the gain. Would all the fortunes in Prydain help my fingers shape a better bowl?"

"There are those," Taran said, half in earnest

as he glanced at the potter's wheel, "who claim work such as yours comes by enchantment."

At this Annlaw threw back his head and laughed heartily. "I wish it did, for it would spare much toil. No, no, Wanderer, my wheel, alas, is like any other. True it is," he added, "that Govannion the Lame, master craftsman of Prydain, long ago fashioned all manner of enchanted implements. He gave them to whom he deemed would use them wisely and well, but one by one they fell into the clutches of Arawn Death-Lord. Now all are gone.

"But Govannion, too, discovered and set down the high secrets of all crafts," Annlaw went on. "These, as well, Arawn stole, to hoard in Annuvin where none may ever profit from them." The potter's face turned grave. "A lifetime have I striven to discover them again, to guess what might have been their nature. Much have I learned—learned by doing, as a child learns to walk. But my steps falter. The deepest lore yet lies beyond my grasp. I fear it ever shall.

"Let me gain this lore," Annlaw said, "and I'll yearn for no magical tools. Let me find the knowledge. And these," he added, holding up his clay-crusted hands, "these will be enough to serve me."

"But you know what you seek," Taran answered. "I, alas, seek without knowing even where to 241 look." He then told Annlaw of Hevydd the Smith and Dwyvach the Weaver-Woman, of the sword and cloak he had made. "I was proud of my work," Taran went on. "Yet, at the end neither anvil nor loom satisfied me."

"What of the potter's wheel?" asked Annlaw. When Taran admitted he knew nothing of this craft and prayed Annlaw to let him see the shaping of clay, the old potter willingly agreed.

Annlaw drew up his coarse robe and seated himself at the wheel, which he quickly set spinning, and on it flung a lump of clay. The potter bent almost humbly to his work, and reached out his hands as tenderly as if he were lifting an unfledged bird. Before Taran's eyes Annlaw began shaping a tall, slender vessel. As Taran stared in awe, the clay seemed to shimmer on the swiftly turning wheel and to change from moment to moment. Now Taran understood Annlaw's words, for indeed between the potter's deft fingers and the clay he saw no separation, as though Annlaw's hands flowed into the clay and gave it life. Annlaw was silent and intent; his lined face had brightened; the years had fallen away from it. Taran felt his heart fill with a joy that seemed to reach from the potter to himself, and in that moment understood that he was in the presence of a true master craftsman, greater than any he had
ever known.

"Fflewddur was wrong," Taran murmured. "If there is enchantment, it lies not in the potter's wheel but in the potter."

"Enchantment there is none," answered Annlaw, never turning from his work. "A gift, perhaps, but a gift that bears with it much toil."

"If I could make a thing of such beauty, it is toil I would welcome," Taran said.

"Sit you down then," said Annlaw, making room for Taran at the wheel. "Shape the clay for yourself." When Taran protested he would spoil Annlaw's half-formed vessel, the potter only laughed. "Spoil it you will, surely. I'll toss it back into the kneading trough, mix it with the other clay, and sooner or later it will serve again. It will not be lost. Indeed, nothing ever is, but comes back in one shape or another."

"But for yourself," Taran said. "The skill you have already put in it will be wasted."

The potter shook his head. "Not so. Craftsmanship isn't like water in an earthen pot, to be taken out by the dipperful until it's empty. No, the more drawn out the more remains. The heart renews itself, Wanderer, and skill grows all the better for it. Here, then. Your hands—thus. Your thumbs—thus."

From the first moment Taran felt the clay whirling beneath his fingers, his heart leaped with the same joy he had seen on the potter's face. The pride of forging his own sword and weaving his own cloak dwindled before this new discovery that made him cry out in sudden delight. But his hands faltered and the clay went awry. Annlaw stopped the wheel. Taran's first vessel was so lopsided and misshapen that, despite his disappointment, he threw back his head and laughed.

Annlaw clapped him on the shoulder. "Well-tried, Wanderer. The first bowl I turned was as ill-favored—and worse. You have the touch for it. But before you learn the craft, you must first learn the clay. Dig, sift, and knead it, know its nature better than that of your closest companion. Then grind pigments for your glazes, understand how the fire of the kiln works upon them."

"Annlaw Clay-Shaper," Taran said in a low voice that hid nothing of his yearning, "will you teach me your craft? This more than all else I long to do."

Annlaw hesitated several moments and looked deeply at Taran. "I can teach you only what you can learn," said the potter. "How much that may be, time will tell. Stay, if that is your wish. Tomorrow we shall begin."

The two wayfarers made themselves comfortable that night in a snug corner of the pottery shed. Gurgi curled on the straw pallet, but Taran sat 244 with knees drawn up and arms clasped about them.

"It's strange," he murmured. "The more of the Commot folk I've known, the fonder have I grown of them. Yet Commot Merin drew me at first sight, closer than all the others." The night was soft and still. Taran smiled wistfully in the darkness. "The moment I saw it, I thought it the one place I'd be content to dwell. And that—that even Eilonwy might have been happy here.

"And at Annlaw's wheel," he went on, "when my hands touched the clay, I knew I would count myself happy to be a potter. More than smithing, more than weaving—it's as though I could speak through my fingers, as though I could give shape to what was in my heart. I understand what Annlaw meant. There is no difference between him and his work. Indeed, Annlaw puts himself into the clay and makes it live with his own life. If I, too, might learn to do this . . ."

Gurgi did not answer. The weary creature was fast asleep. Taran smiled and drew the cloak over Gurgi's shoulders. "Sleep well," he said. "We may have come to the end of our journey."

Annlaw was as good as his word. In the days that followed, the potter showed Taran skills no less important than the working of the clay itself: the finding of proper earths, judging their texture and

245

quality, sifting, mixing, tempering. Gurgi joined Taran in all the tasks, and soon his shaggy hair grew so crusted with dust, mud, and gritty glaze that he looked like an unbaked clay pot set on a pair of skinny legs.

The summer sped quickly and happily, and the more Taran saw the potter at his craft the more he marveled. At the kneading trough, Annlaw pounded the clay with greater vigor than Hevydd the Smith at his anvil; and at the wheel did the most intricate work with a deftness surpassing even that of Dwyvach the Weaver-Woman. As early as he rose in the mornings, Taran always found the potter already up and about his tasks. Annlaw was tireless, often spending nights without sleep and days without food, absorbed in labor at his wheel. Seldom was the potter content to repeat a pattern, but strove to better even what he himself had originated.

"Stale water is a poor drink," said Annlaw. "Stale skill is worse. And the man who walks in his own footsteps only ends where he began."

Not until autumn did Annlaw let Taran try his hand at the wheel again. This time, the bowl Taran shaped was not as ill-formed as the other.

Annlaw, studying it carefully, nodded his head and told him, "You have learned a little, Wanderer." Nevertheless, to Taran's dismay, Annlaw cast 246 the bowl into the kneading trough. "Never fear," said the potter. "When you shape one worth the keeping, it will be fired in the kiln."

Though Taran feared such a time might never come, it was not long before Annlaw judged a vessel, a shallow bowl simple in design yet well-proportioned, to be ready for firing. He set it, along with other pots and bowls he had crafted for the folk of Commot Isav, into a kiln taller and deeper than Hevydd's furnace. While Annlaw calmly turned to finishing other vessels for the Commot folk, Taran's anxiety grew until he felt that he himself was baking in the flames. But at last, when the firing was done and the pieces had cooled, the potter drew out the bowl, turned it around in his hands as Taran waited breathlessly, and tapped it with a clay-rimmed finger.

He grinned at Taran. "It rings true. Beginner's work, Wanderer, but not to be ashamed of."

Taran's heart lifted as if he had fashioned a wine bowl handsomer than ever Lord Gast had seen.

But his joy changed soon to despair. Through autumn Taran shaped other vessels; yet, to his growing dismay, none satisfied him, none matched his hopes, despite the painful toil he poured into the work.

"What lacks?" he cried to Annlaw. "I could forge a sword well enough and weave a cloak well enough. But now, what I truly long to grasp is beyond my reach. Must the one skill I sought above all be denied me?" he burst out in an anguished voice. "Is the gift forbidden me?" He bowed his head, and his heart froze even as he spoke the words, for he knew, within himself, he had touched the truth.

Annlaw did not gainsay him, but only looked at him for a long while with deep sadness.

"Why?" Taran whispered. "Why is this so?"

"It is a heavy question," Annlaw replied at last. He put a hand on Taran's shoulder. "Indeed, no man can answer it. There are those who have labored all their lives to gain the gift, striving until the end only to find themselves mistaken; and those who had it born in them yet never knew; those who lost heart too soon; and those who should never have begun at all.

"Count yourself lucky," the potter went on, "that you have understood this now and not spent your years in vain hope. This much have you learned, and no learning is wasted."

"What then shall I do?" Taran asked. Grief and bitterness such as he had known in Craddoc's valley flooded over him.

"There are more ways to happiness than in the shaping of a pot," replied Annlaw. "You have been happy in Merin. You still can be. There is work

for you to do. Your help is welcome and valuable to

me, as a friend as much as an apprentice. Why, look you now," he went on in a cheerful tone, "tomorrow I would send my ware to Commot Isav. But a day's journey is long for one of my years. As a friend, will you bear the burden for me?"

Taran nodded. "I will carry your ware to Isav." He turned away, knowing that his happiness was ended, like a flawed vessel shattered in the firing.

CHAPTER XX

The Spoilers

ext morning, as Taran had promised, he loaded Melynlas and Gurgi's pony with the potter's ware and, Gurgi beside him, set out for Commot Isav. Annlaw, he knew, could as well have sent word to the Commot folk, asking them to come and bear away their own vessels.

"This is not an errand I do for him, but a kindness he does for me," Taran told Gurgi. "I think he means to give me time to myself, to find my own thoughts. As for that," he added sorrowfully, "so far I've found none. I long to stay in Merin, yet there's little to keep me here. I prize Annlaw as my friend and as a master of his craft. But his craft will never be mine."

Still pondering and troubled at heart Taran reached Isav some while before dusk. It was the smallest Commot of all he had seen, with fewer than half-a-dozen cottages and a little grazing plot for a handful of sheep and cattle. A knot of men were gathered by the sheepfold. As Taran rode closer he saw their faces tightly drawn and grim.

Perplexed at this he called out his name and told them he brought pottery from Annlaw Clay-Shaper.

"Greetings to you," said one man, naming himself as Drudwas Son of Pebyr. "And farewell in the same breath," he added. "Our thanks to Annlaw and yourself. But stay to share our hospitality and you may stay to shed your blood.

"Outlaws rove the hills," Drudwas went on quickly, answering Taran's questioning frown, "a band, perhaps a dozen strong. We have heard they plundered two Commots already, and not content were they with a sheep or cow for their own food, but slaughtered all the herd for the joy of it. Today, not long past, I saw horsemen over the rise, and leading them a yellow-haired ruffian on a sorrel mare."

"Dorath!" Taran cried.

"How then?" asked one of the Commot men. "Do you know this band?"

"If it's Dorath's Company, I know them well enough," Taran answered. "They are paid swords; and if none will hire them, I judge them glad to kill even without fee. Hard warriors they are, as I have seen them, and cruel as the Huntsmen of Annuvin."

Drudwas nodded gravely. "So it is said. It   251

may be they will pass us by," he went on, "but this I doubt. Commot Isav is small prey, but where defenders are few the reasons to attack are all the more."

Taran glanced at the men. From their faces and bearing he knew their courage would not lack; but once more he heard Dorath's laughter and recalled the man's cunning and ruthlessness. "And if they attack," he asked, "what shall you do?"

"What would you have us do?" Drudwas angrily burst out. "Offer tribute and beg them to spare us? Give our animals to their swords and our homes to their torches? Commot Isav has ever been at peace; our pride is husbandry not warfare. But we mean to stand against them. Have we better choice?"

"I can ride back to Merin," Taran replied, "and bring you help."

"Too far and too long," Drudwas answered. "Nor would I do so, even then, for it would leave Merin ill-defended. No, we stand as we are. Against twelve, seven. My son Llassar," he began, indicating a tall, eager-faced boy scarcely older than Taran had been when Coll first dubbed him Assistant Pig-Keeper.

"Your count is amiss," Taran interrupted. "You are not seven, but nine. Gurgi and I stand with you."

Drudwas shook his head. "You owe us no service or duty, Wanderer. We welcome your swords, but will not ask for them."

"They are yours nonetheless," Taran replied, and Gurgi nodded agreement. "Will you heed me? Nine may stand against a dozen and win the day. But with Dorath, number counts less than skill. Were he alone I would still fear him as much as twelve. He will fight shrewdly and strive to gain the most at least cost. We must answer him in kind." The Commot men listened carefully as Taran then spoke of a ruse to make the raiders believe themselves outnumbered, and to attack where Dorath would expect no more than feeble defense.

"If two men were to lie waiting in the sheepfold and two in the cattle pen, ready to spring up," Taran said, "they might take the band unawares and hold them a few moments while the rest of us attack from ambush in the rear. At the same time, if the women of your households set up a din with rakes and hoes, it would seem other swordsmen had hastened to join us."

Drudwas thought a long moment, then nodded. "Your plan may be sound, Wanderer. But I fear for those in the pens, as they must bear the brunt for all of us. If aught should go awry, small chance of escape would they have."

"I shall be one to keep watch in the sheepfold," Taran began.

"And I the other," Llassar broke in quickly.

Drudwas frowned. "I would not spare you because you are my son. You are a good lad and gentle with the flock. I think of your years . . ."

"The flock is in my charge," Llassar cried. "By right my place is with the Wanderer."

The men spoke hurriedly among themselves, at last agreeing that Llassar would keep watch with Taran, while Drudwas stood guard over the cattle along with Gurgi who, fearful though he was, refused to be any farther from Taran's side. By the time all plans were set and the Commot men posted among the trees just beyond the sheepfold, a full moon had risen above thin clouds. The cold light sharpened the edges of the shadows and the outlines of brush and branches. In the fold Taran and Llassar crouched amid the restless flock.

For a time neither spoke. In the bright moonlight the face of Llassar seemed to Taran more boyish than before; he saw the youth was afraid and making all effort to hide it. Though uneasy himself, he grinned assuringly at Llassar. Drudwas had been right. The boy was young, untried. And yet—Taran smiled, knowing that he himself, at Llassar's age, would have claimed the same right.

"Your plan is good, Wanderer," Llassar said at

last in a hushed voice, speaking, Taran knew, more

to ease his own disquiet than anything else. "Better than we should have done. It cannot fail."

"All plans can fail," Taran said, almost harshly. He fell silent then. Fears had begun stirring in him like leaves in a chill wind. Sweat drenched his body under the fleece jacket. He had come to Isav unknown, unproven, yet the men of the Commot had willingly heeded him and willingly put their fate in his hands. They had accepted his plan when another might have served better; should it fail, though all their lives could be forfeit, the blame would be his alone. He gripped the hilt of his sword and strained his eyes to peer into the darkness. There was no movement, and even the shadows seemed frozen.

"You are called Wanderer," Llassar went on quietly, with some shyness. "To my mind, one who wanders must as well be one who seeks. Is this true?"

Taran shook his head. "I sought once to be a smith and once to be a weaver. And once a potter. But that is over. Now, perhaps I must wander without seeking."

"If you seek nothing," Llassar said with a friendly laugh, "then you have little chance of finding it. Our life is not easy here," he went on. "It is not willingness that lacks, but knowledge. The Sons of Don have long held Prydain against the Lord of Annuvin, and for their protection we are grateful;

yet the secrets Arawn Death-Lord stole from us—to regain them, my father says, would give us stouter shield and sword than even the battle hosts of Prince Gwydion himself. But for all that, Isav is my home and I am well-content in it." Llassar grinned. "I do not envy you, Wanderer."

Taran did not answer for a time. Then he murmured, "No, it is I who envy you."

They said no more, listening alertly to every sound as the night wore away and the moon, fading behind thickening clouds, lost shape and its light spread like pale mist. In a while Llassar blew out his breath in relief. "They will not come," he said. "They will pass us by."

Even as he spoke, the darkness shattered in fragments that turned into the figures of armed warriors. Taran sprang to his feet as the gate burst open.

Taran sounded his battle horn, then flung himself upon the warrior who cried out in surprise and stumbled backward. Llassar had leaped up at the same instant as Taran, and the shepherd plunged against the press of the attackers at the gate, thrusting with his spear. Taran struck out blindly, struggling not only against the raiders but against the sudden terror that his plan had failed, that the outlaws had come too silently, too swiftly. In another moment, above the frantic bleating of the frightened animals, a great shout burst from the Commot men as they rose from the cover of the trees, and from the huts came the clash of iron upon iron.

At the sheepfold the outlaws hesitated. Llassar's opponent had fallen. Taran glimpsed the boy spring past him and strike again with his spear. The attack wavered at the gate, as the raiders turned their weapons against the men of Isav. But one warrior, growling like a wild beast, long knife upraised, raced into the pen as if to wreak all the destruction he could, and Taran grappled with the man who spun about and slashed at him. It was Gloff.

The warrior recognized him; Gloff's first astonishment changed to an ugly grin almost of pleasure and eagerness, as he shifted the knife in his hand. Gloff lunged and Taran flung up his weapon to ward against the blow. But the warrior leaped forward, his free hand clawing at Taran's eyes, and his blade flickered as its point drove swiftly in a killing stroke. A figure plunged between them. It was Llassar. Taran shouted a warning as the boy strove to catch the blow on his spear shaft. Snarling, Gloff turned his attack and struck viciously at Llassar. The shepherd fell. With a cry of rage Taran raised his sword. Suddenly, Drudwas was beside him. Gloff shrieked as the blade of the husbandman chopped downward.

Under the onslaught of the Commot folk Dorath's warriors fell back. Amid the turmoil of racing men Taran found himself borne away from the fold. Daring a backward glance he could glimpse neither Drudwas nor Llassar; in fury, he pressed onward. Torches flared, and he saw that the women and girls of Isav had joined their men, flailing with hoes, rakes, and pitchforks at the raiders. Taran cast about for Gurgi and shouted his name, but his voice was drowned in the tumult.

A fierce bellowing had risen from the cattle pen as a dark shape burst through the bars. Taran gasped in astonishment to see a furious black bull heaving and plunging among the raiders. On its back clung Gurgi, yelling at the top of his voice, kicking his heels against the powerful animal's flanks, turning its charge against the terrified remainder of Dorath's band.

"They flee!" shouted one of the Commot men.

Taran pressed ahead. The raiders, who had left their mounts at the fringe of trees, now hastened to gain them, caught between the Commot folk and the slashing horns of the enraged bull. Taran glimpsed Dorath astride the sorrel mare and ran to overtake him. But Dorath spurred the steed and galloped into the wood.

Taran turned and raced to the stables, whistling for Melynlas. One of the Commot men caught at his arm and cried, "The day is ours, Wanderer!"

Only then did Taran realize the sounds of the fray had ceased. Dorath himself had vanished. Taran hurried to the sheepfold where the wife of Drudwas knelt, her arms about her son.

"Llassar!" Taran cried in dismay, dropping beside the shepherd. The boy's eyes opened and he strove to grin at Taran.

"His wound is not deep," said Drudwas. "He will live to tend his flock."

"And so I will," Llassar said to Taran, "and thanks to you, I'll have a flock to tend."

Taran put a hand on the boy's shoulder. "And to you," he answered, "to you I owe much more than sheep."

"Full half the band will plunder no longer," said Drudwas, "neither Commot Isav nor any Commot. The rest are scattered, and it will be long before their wounds heal. You have well served us, Wanderer, you and your companion. You came among us strangers. We count you strangers no longer, but friends."

CHAPTER XXI

The Mirror

Although the folk of Isav urged him to linger, Taran took leave of them and rode slowly back to Merin. The defeat of Dorath's Company held no savor, for his thoughts still turned restlessly; his questions still found no answers; and he was more downhearted than ever. To Annlaw he said little of his deeds in Isav, and it was Gurgi, bursting with pride, who told what had befallen them.

"Yes, yes!" cried Gurgi. "Wicked robbers fled with yellings! Oh, they feared kindly master. And feared bold Gurgi, too! And great bull with stampings and trampings, sharp horns with jabbings and stabbings!"

"You should be well-content, Wanderer," Annlaw said to Taran, who had remained silent all the while. "You've saved honest folk their lives and homes."

"Drudwas told me I was no stranger, but a friend. For that I am glad," Taran answered. "I only wish," he added, "that I weren't a stranger to myself.

What use am I?" he burst out. "To myself, to anyone? None that I can see."

"The folk of Isav would gainsay you," the potter answered. "And there might be others who would welcome a stout blade and a bold heart."

"A hired sword?" Taran replied bitterly. "And follow the same way as Dorath?" He shook his head. "When I was a child I dreamed of adventure, glory, of honor in feats of arms. I think now that these things are shadows."

"If you see them as shadows then you see them for what they are," Annlaw agreed. "Many have pursued honor, and in the pursuit lost more of it than ever they could gain. But I did not mean a hired sword . . ." He stopped abruptly and was thoughtful a moment. "To see them for what they are," he murmured, returning to his first words. "Perhaps—perhaps . . ." The potter looked closely at Taran.

"The Commot lore tells how one may see himself for what he is. Whether it be true or no more than an old wives' tale I will not judge," the potter went on slowly. "But the lore says that he who would know himself need only gaze in the Mirror of Llunet."

Though Annlaw had spoken quietly, Taran heard the potter's words like a thunderclap.

"The Mirror of Llunet?" Taran cried. Since

leaving Craddoc's valley he had put away all thought of the Mirror, hidden and forgotten it, and the days had covered it as dead leaves on a burial mound. "The Mirror," he repeated in a stifled voice, "the goal of my quest from the beginning. I had given up searching. Now do I find it when I seek it least of all?"

"Your quest?" Annlaw said, perplexed. He had risen and was watching Taran with concern. "Of this you have told me nothing, Wanderer."

"I would have no pride in the telling," Taran replied.

But now, as Annlaw listened quietly, a look of kindness on his face, little by little Taran was able to speak of Caer Dallben, of Orddu, of where the quest had led him, of Craddoc's death and his own despair. "Once," Taran concluded, "I would have asked nothing better than to find the Mirror. Now, even if it were in my hand, I would dread to look in it."

"I understand your fears," the potter answered quietly. "The Mirror may put your heart at ease—or trouble you all the more. Such is the risk. The choice must be yours.

"But know this, Wanderer," Annlaw went on, as Taran bit his lips in silence, "it is not such a mirror as you think. It lies close by here in the Llawgadarn Mountains, no more than two days' distance, in a cave at the head of the Lake of Llunet. The Mirror of Llunet is a pool of water."

"A pool of water?" Taran cried. "What enchantment gives it power? For enchanted it must be."

"It is," answered the potter, "to those who deem it so."

"What of yourself?" Taran asked in a low voice. "Have you sought to look in it?"

"That I have not," replied Annlaw. "For I well know who I am. Annlaw Clay-Shaper. For better or worse, that knowledge must serve me my lifetime."

"And I," Taran murmured, "what knowledge will serve mine?" He said nothing for a time. At last he raised his head. "It is true. I fear to look in the Mirror, and fear to know what it might tell me. But I have already known shame," he flung out bitterly. "Must I know cowardice as well?

"In the morning," Taran continued, "in the morning I journey to the Mirror of Llunet."

His decision gave him little comfort. At first light, as he and Gurgi saddled their mounts, his doubts chilled him more than the cold mist of late autumn. Nevertheless, having made his choice he set a swift pace, riding northward from Merin to the Llawgadarn Mountains, taking his bearings on the high peak of Mount Meledin, for it was at the foot of

Meledin, as Annlaw told him, that he would find the cave. The companions rode silently and steadily, halting only when the day had so far waned they could no longer guide the steeds along the paths. They camped on the soft carpet of pine needles, but a deep uneasiness had settled on the two wayfarers and they slept little.

At dawn of the next day they gathered up their gear and rode at a good pace along the crest of a ridge. Soon Taran called out and pointed downward. The Lake of Llunet stretched in a long oval, gleaming in the early sun. Its waters were calm, blue, and the Lake itself seemed a perfect mirror that held the tree-lined shore in its depths. At some distance Mount Meledin rose, tall but seeming almost weightless in the mist still clinging to its long slopes.

Taran's heart beat faster as the companions made their way downward to the shore. Closer to Meledin the land fell in sharp drops, and short stretches of meadow broke into shallow ravines. Near a stream tumbling from the upper reaches of the mountain the companions tethered their steeds. Taran had already sighted the cave and hastened toward it, with Gurgi scrambling after him.

"There!" Taran cried. "There! The Mirror!"

At the foot of Meledin wind and weather had
carved an arching cave little more than a few paces

deep. Rivulets trickled from the moss-grown rocks of its overhanging brow. Taran raced toward it. His heart pounded; his pulse burnt in his wrists. Yet as he drew closer his pace slowed, and fear weighed heavy as a chain about his legs. At the mouth of the cave he halted a long moment. Gurgi glanced anxiously at him.

"It is here," Taran murmured. He stepped forward.

Within, a shallow basin hollowed in the floor of smooth stones, lay the Mirror of Llunet like a shield of polished silver, gleaming of itself despite the shadows. Taran slowly knelt at the rim. The basin held no more than a finger's depth of water, fed drop by drop from a thread of moisture twining down the rocky wall. The passing of countless years had not filled it to the brim. Yet shallow though it was, the water seemed a depthless crystal whose facets turned one upon the other, each catching brilliant beams of white.

Scarcely daring to breathe lest he trouble the shining surface, Taran bent closer. The cave was utterly silent, and it seemed that even the falling of a wisp of dry moss would shatter the reflection. His hands trembled as he saw his own face, travel-worn and sun-scorched. With all his heart he longed to turn away, but forced himself to look more deeply. Were his eyes playing tricks on him? Closer he knelt. 265

What he saw made him cry out in disbelief.

At the same instant Gurgi shrieked in terror. Taran leaped to his feet and spun around as Gurgi ran and cowered at his side. Before him stood Dorath.

The man's face was stubble-bearded, his dirty yellow hair hung into his eyes. The horsehide jacket was slashed along one side and mud crusted his boots. In one hand he held food which he scooped up with his fingers and crammed into his mouth. He grinned at Taran.

"Well met, Lord Swineherd," Dorath said between mouthfuls.

"Ill-met, Dorath," Taran cried, drawing his sword. "Will you call your Company to set upon us? Call them, then, all who fled us at Commot Isav!" He raised the weapon and strode forward.

Dorath laughed harshly. "Will you strike before my own blade is out?"

"Draw it, then," Taran flung back at him.

"So I shall, when my meal is done," Dorath said. He gave a scornful grunt. "Your blade is ill-favored, swineherd, uglier than Gloff's face." He grinned slyly. "Mine is the fairer weapon, yet gained at no cost. My Company?" he added. "Would you have me call them? They are deaf. For half of them, the dirt of their graves stops their ears. I saw you at

Isav, and guessed it was you who rallied the Commot clods. Alas, I had no time to linger and pay my greetings to you."

Dorath wiped his mouth on the back of his hand. "Of those who rode from Isav, two cowards fled and I've seen none of them. Two were heavily wounded. Those, I myself sped on their journey to the carrion crows, and they burden me no longer. But no matter. I'll soon find others to join me.

"Meantime, so much the better," he went on. "I'll share your treasure with none but myself."

"Treasure?" Taran cried. "There is no treasure! Draw your blade, Dorath, or I'll kill you unarmed as you'd have done to me."

"An end to your lying, swineherd," Dorath growled. "Do you still take me for a fool? I've known of your travels, and the bent path you followed here did not deceive me. Your saddlebags hold nothing of worth; I've seen that for myself. So the prize is yet to be claimed."

He strode to the Mirror. "Is this your trove? What have you found, swineherd? A mud puddle? What does it hide?"

Taran cried out, though before he could fling himself upon Dorath the warrior stamped his heavy boot into the pool and, with a curse, sent the water spurting from the basin.

"It holds nothing!" Dorath burst out, his face twisting in rage.

Taran gasped and stumbled forward. Dorath drew his sword.

"My meal is ended, swineherd," Dorath cried.

He struck heavily and the force of his onslaught sent Taran reeling from the cave. Gurgi yelled in fury and clutched at the warrior, who seized him with a powerful grasp and dashed him against the rocky wall. Snarling, Dorath sprang after Taran.

Scrambling to his feet, Taran brought up his blade to meet the warrior's attack. Dorath spat and lunged again, driving Taran toward the slope. As the warrior bore closer upon him, Taran lost his footing, stumbled backward, and dropped to one knee.

With a mocking laugh Dorath raised his weapon, and Taran saw the blade that once had been his own glint sharply as Dorath swung it down with all his strength. Taran saw his death upon him and flung up his sword in a last attempt to ward against the blow.

The blades met with a grating, ringing clash. Taran's weapon shuddered in his hand, the shock threw him to earth. Yet his blade held. The sword of Dorath shattered on it.

Cursing, Dorath flung the useless hilt at Taran's face, turned and ran to the cover of pines along the shore. Hearing her master's whistle, Dorath's sorrel mare broke from the trees. Taran sprang to pursue the fleeing warrior.

"Help, help!" Gurgi's voice cried from the cave. "Kindly master! Oh, help wounded Gurgi!"

Hearing this Taran halted even as Dorath leaped astride his mount and galloped away. Taran raced to the cave. Within, Gurgi moaned and tried to sit up. Taran knelt quickly and saw the creature's forehead was heavily gashed, but that Gurgi's pain came more from terror than from his hurts. He carried him from the cave and propped him against a boulder.

Taran did not return to the Mirror of Llunet. Already he had seen it empty, its spattered water spread over the stones, holding only the muddy print of Dorath's boot. He sank down beside Gurgi and put his head in his hands. For long he did not move or speak.

"Come," he said at last, helping Gurgi to his feet. "Come. We have far to journey."

A light glowed in Annlaw's hut. The night was nearly spent, yet Taran saw the potter still bent over his wheel.

Annlaw rose to his feet as Taran slowly crossed the threshold. Neither spoke for some while. The potter anxiously studied Taran's face, and said at last, "Have you looked into the Mirror, Wanderer?"

Taran nodded. "For a few moments. But none 269

shall look in it again. It is destroyed." He told of Dorath and the happenings at the Lake of Llunet. When Taran had done, the potter sadly shook his head.

"You saw nothing then?" said Annlaw.

"I learned what I sought to learn," Taran replied.

"I will not question you, Wanderer," said Annlaw. "But if it is in your heart to tell me, I will listen."

"I saw myself," Taran answered. "In the time I watched, I saw strength—and frailty. Pride and vanity, courage and fear. Of wisdom, a little. Of folly, much. Of intentions, many good ones; but many more left undone. In this, alas, I saw myself a man like any other.

"But this, too, I saw," he went on. "Alike as men may seem, each is different as flakes of snow, no two the same. You told me you had no need to seek the Mirror, knowing you were Annlaw Clay-Shaper. Now I know who I am: myself and none other. I am Taran."

Annlaw did not reply immediately. Then he said, "If you have learned this you have learned the deepest secret the Mirror could tell you. Perhaps it was truly enchanted after all."

"There was no enchantment," Taran answered. He smiled. "It was a pool of water, the most beautiful I have seen. But a pool of water, no more than that.

"At first," he went on, "I thought Orddu had sent a fool on a fool's errand. She did not. She meant me to see what the Mirror showed me. Any stream, any river would have given me the same reflection, but I would not have understood it then as I understand it now.

"As for my parentage," he added, "it makes little difference. True kinship has naught to do with blood ties, however strong they be. I think we are all kin, brothers and sisters one to the other, all children of all parents. And the birthright I once sought, I seek it no longer. The folk of the Free Commots taught me well, that manhood is not given but earned. Even King Smoit in Cantrev Cadiffor told me this, but I did not heed him.

"Llonio said life was a net for luck; to Hevydd the Smith life was a forge; and to Dwyvach the Weaver-Woman a loom. They spoke truly, for it is all of these. But you," Taran said, his eyes meeting the potter's, "you have shown me life is one thing more. It is clay to be shaped, as raw clay on a potter's wheel."

Annlaw nodded. "And you, Wanderer, how will you shape your clay?"

"I cannot stay in Merin," Taran replied, "much as I love it. Caer Dallben waits for me, as it 271 has always waited. My life is there, and gladly I return to it, for I have been too long away."

They sat silently then: Taran, Gurgi, and Annlaw Clay-Shaper. As dawn lightened, Taran clasped the potter's hand and bade him farewell.

"Good journey to you, Wanderer," called Annlaw, as Taran swung astride Melynlas. "Do not forget us, for we shall not forget you."

"I have the sword I fashioned," Taran proudly cried, "the cloak I wove, and the bowl I shaped. And the friendship of those in the fairest land of Prydain. No man can find greater treasure."

Melynlas pawed the ground, impatient, and Taran gave the stallion rein.

Thus Taran rode from Merin with Gurgi at his side.

And as he did, it seemed he could hear voices calling to him. "Remember us! Remember us!" He turned once, but Merin was far behind and out of sight. From the hills a wind had risen, driving the scattered leaves before it, bearing homeward to Caer Dallben. Taran followed it.